what

changes everything

UNBRIDLED BOOKS

what
changes everything

masha hamilton

Unbridled Books

Library of Congress Cataloging-in-Publication Data

Hamilton, Masha.
What changes everything / Masha Hamilton.
p. cm.
ISBN 978-1-60953-091-4
1. Afghan War, 2001—Casualties—Fiction.   2. Veterans'
families—United States—Fiction.   3. Life change events—Fiction.
4. Families—Afghanistan—Fiction.   5. Epistolary fiction.   I. Title.
PS3558.A44338W48 2013
813'.54—dc23
2012039096

1   3   5   7   9   10   8   6   4   2

Book Design by SH • CV

First Printing

For those who were changed

part one

You don't need a war.

You don't need to go anywhere.

It's a myth: if you hurl

Yourself at chaos

Chaos will catch you.

— ELIZA GRISWOLD

Beirut. Baghdad. Sarajevo.

Bethlehem. Kabul. Not of

course here.

— ADRIENNE RICH

Najibullah

Letter to My Daughters I

September 3rd, 1996

destiny is a saddled ass, my daughters; he goes where you lead him. But you must know the rules to discern the path. First, give full trust to no one. The smiling horseman with whom you bow for dawn prayers may seek to kill you by nightfall. Work in cooperation, of course— what dust would rise from one rider alone? But do not let your lashes slip lazily to your cheeks while the sun remains in the sky. Whatever Allah wills shall be. Nevertheless, tie your steed's knees tight before sleeping.

It is dawn just after prayers; Kabul's golden light creeps in through my window, a timid but relentless thief here to steal the night, and I am imagining you three with me instead of in Delhi, us all cross-legged on toshaks, looking directly into each other's faces. My mind has become so practiced in seeing you where you are not, in fact, that I can almost hear you teasing me now—horsemen? Steeds? You would tell me, if you could, that these are male metaphors, and male concerns.

But you've been raised liberated girls; your dealings will be with both genders. Besides, though perhaps it is less likely, a woman too may pat your back with a blade in her palm.

I have barely slept the night thinking of you girls and your mother. As *reports reach me of the fundamentalists clawing daily closer to Kabul, the courage that buffered me as Afghanistan's president bolsters me still. I believe these extremists, being fellow Pashtuns, will at last send me into exile, which means I will rejoin my family.*

Nevertheless, as it is hard to predict where a worn fighter's bullet will land, there is urgency to my task. For over four years and four months, I have been unable to share a meal with you, hear in person of your plans or tell of mine. We have not played a single game of Ping-Pong nor watched a movie together. When I think of it, as I do often, my eyes feel rubbed with salt, my throat thickened with mud, my chest pummeled by an angry fist. I put these lessons in writing to be sure you will have them in case you need them before we are reunited.

So, then, the rules. When you must trust someone, rely on a stranger more easily than on a friend; yes, because a friend knows your soft spots. But remember, family is the marrow of your bones. Who is here with me still? My two UN "guards" and a young Pashtun, Amin, who waits on me. But my daily companion, the one with whom I share my deepest thoughts, is my brother Shahpur, your kaakaa jan. Together we follow politics and watch television and talk of you. Shahpur celebrated—but that's not the right word without you—he marked my forty-ninth birthday last month, a hard day to be apart from my beloved wife and girls. He holds me upright in your absence. You sisters, too, will lift each other when the need appears.

Take care of your mother-flower until I return to you. I became her tutor all those years ago driven by the hope that she would fall in love with me over formulas and test questions. They can arrest or exile me—I will always be a lucky man because of her. She gave me you three, and a home of laughter even in dark times, and the strong foundation that has allowed me to do my work.

And this rule: love your country. Victim of many men's fury, corrupted by fanatics who believe our landlocked status means we sit in the cup of their hands, it still remains proud. "I come to you and my heart finds rest," Ahmed Shah Baba wrote of our motherland. "Away from you, grief clings to my heart like a snake." I know your memories of Afghanistan will be tinged by our separation and my detention. But put that aside, learn our history, and return one day to make your own impact.

Remember that Afghanistan must be one united nation, all ethnic divisions discarded. Remember the couplet of the great Pashtun poet and warrior Khushal Khan Khattak: "Sail through vast oceans as long as you can, oh whale, for in small brooks I can predict your decay!"

Remember, also, Khan Abdul Ghaffar Khan. He too endured house arrest. He too knew it possible to be a devout Muslim and still support a progressive society. His goal, to unite all, was noble. Together one day, we'll visit his resting place in Jalalabad.

Be brave. Be proud.

Fear and shame are father and son, and you should feel neither. You will need courage to meet detractors—the strong or outspoken always have those who would malign them. Still, we Afghans are raised on bravery with our morning chai; *I remind you that it runs easily through our blood.*

Be punctual. Work hard. Memorize the Quran. Don't forget your Dari. Never boast: it is the small mouth that speaks big words.

Do not believe the stories you hear about me, my daughters. At least, not wholly. You are still so young—Muski only eight years old—but I know grim murmurs make their way to your ears already; your mother tells me. If I was a puppet, how did I manage to hold on to power for three years after the Soviets scuttled away? If I drew blood, it was only in self-defense or for Afghanistan. If it was I who was the roadblock to peace, then why has our city been ravaged by warfare in the months and years since I left office? Do you remember Kharabat Street, its musicians flinging open their doors to compete for the chance to perform at the palace, their heart-thumping music expanding and floating into the mountains? Massoud's single-note rockets left the Street of the Musicians in rubble. Districts where you three and your mother used to walk are now impassable, proof enough that I preserved peace, not obstructed it.

And now your uncle is at my door. I will write you again soon—not a diary, since when the days are filled with events that might make an interesting diary there is not a spare moment to record them, and those are not my circumstances now. Instead, my enemies have given me the gift of time. As a satellite phone is available too infrequently for my wishes, I will make for you a written record of the state of your father's mind during this fifth year living as "Honored Guest" while our fractious country and its devious leaders struggle forward without my firm hand. I will ask the boy Amin to send these off discreetly, since I want no UN censor marring my pages.

Soon, inshallah, I will rejoin you. Until then, with love for you, and a country of kisses for your mother, my dearest Fati,

Najib

Amin

*a*min spread his rug on the ground behind the office and then parted his lips to inhale fully. A crippled sparrow stood in stingy bush-shade and watched. Smoke and exhaust threaded through Kabul's air, and the city's tensions pressed against the compound walls; nevertheless, nothing matched performing *salat* under an open sky, even if sometimes the closeness to Allah made him feel that much more ashamed. He raised his hands next to his ears, crossed his arms, paused, and then bent at the waist; he straightened, he bowed, he lowered his forehead to the earth in a dance of sacred ritual by now burrowed deep in muscle memory. He had first prayed as a child beside his father, mimicking the traditional movements in time to words of supplication. These days his own son often stood next to him, and so at its best, prayer connected him not only to his God but to his past, his future, his people.

At its best. When he wasn't preoccupied, that is. September was his month of regret, the month when his mind willfully wandered.

As the sparrow hopped closer, he took measure of his regret; he found it hadn't shrunk over the last year, even though he'd been a good man, or tried. Goodness wasn't simply a matter of intention;

life conspired to sidetrack the well-meaning, and somehow doing right by those you loved most always proved far more complicated than being kind to strangers—as if the two, love and complications, had to be ingested in equal measure. He had long ago realized that the unintended sins of the virtuous caused the worst damage: sins committed when one should have known better, or tried harder, or spoken up or stayed silent.

"They will never know how fiercely I wish I could stand before them—before *you*—and ask forgiveness." Amin could have said those words, though they belonged to Najib. Even in the middle of it, Amin had known it as an exceptional moment in his life. What he couldn't see then was what it would cost him. He'd been so young. He'd do it differently now, of course. Another chance was not to be had.

Nor another chance at this day's noon prayers. Najib could be considered later. Lowering his forehead again to the prayer rug, he wordlessly asked Allah's forgiveness for his break in attention, cleared his mind, and offered praise for the Master of the Judgment Day, the Powerful One of ninety-nine names.

Clarissa

September 3rd

C larissa pressed the "end" button on the phone's receiver. Its quiet click made her think of everyday conclusions: a door closing, a bridge rising, the halting of a heart. She saw out the window that night had choked off the Brooklyn sky while she'd been talking to her husband half a world away. Her *new* husband, as she still thought of him—though they'd been married almost three years, "husband" was not a word that fell easily from her lips.

She didn't want to feel irritated with him. She dropped her tensed shoulders and shook her hands as if to release the memory of long miles, missed connections, censored language. She never liked to argue long-distance—not with a friend, not with her brother, certainly not with this man she'd married. Robbed of touch or expression, words became easily knotted.

Besides, life should not be disrupted so near to sleep. Leave it for another day. She was forty-two; she knew how to compartmentalize by this time, didn't she?

Urban gray lay beyond the window, with shadows and sirens and complicated nighttime intentions. She turned back toward the humdrum solidity of the lit kitchen: a table messy with notes for her study on the urban history of Detroit; yogurt, cranberry juice, and spinach in the fridge; a bottle of calcium pills on the counter next to a scrawled note from her stepdaughter to her husband, weeks old now. A coffee machine still partly filled with day-old brew, a radio quietly broadcasting unalarming news. She welcomed these particulars that were the bones of her current life, but she did not pause to treasure them. There it is, then, the human tragedy: failure to celebrate the plain pillow that catches one's head each night.

Mandy

September 4th

kabul from above was a panoramic movie—sensual sand rivers, thirsty cracks diving into the earth, a disembodied pilot's voice reciting *Allahu Akbar* three times on final approach, a prayer that the flight attendant failed to translate into English. But once Mandy had landed and had entered the airport's squat and tawdry buildings, the city abruptly seemed less romantic, emitting the scent of the dangerously foreign: dark and masculine musk. Mandy fought off a knife-like wave of fear. What was she? A middle-aged woman with a pale face and secret hopes, unnaturally adjusting her headscarf: she didn't belong. She had a sudden vision of high school dances—those petri dishes of adolescent insecurities, still mildly painful three decades later. Even though she'd been considered "popular," she'd known it to be a disguise that couldn't provide permanent cover-up, a mask in constant danger of slipping. Each time she'd entered that dolled-up lunchroom with its streamers and strobe lights and a band playing piercingly in a corner, she'd imagined everyone would finally notice the "Outsider" tattooed on her forehead.

Here, however, no one seemed to pay attention to her at all. On

the airplane, men had watched her through slitted eyes at once def-
erential and bold, and other women had smiled shyly. Now everyone
was far too involved in the business of pushing their way into the
terminal or fighting their way to the exit. The lights appeared to
have burned out, or maybe the electricity had shut off: the terminal
was in shadows, and Mandy saw, as they inched forward, that the
baggage carousel stood silent and still. A half-dozen men hustled in,
pulling luggage on flat carts, shouting out unknown words and gesturing for everyone to *clear a path, clear a path*, and then dumping
bags onto the stranded carousel as if they expected it to involuntarily
leap to life. Passengers of both genders pushed their way toward the
heap, the women gaining momentum whenever a man leapt back to
avoid physical contact.

In this adamant rush of activity, Mandy hesitated. What to do
now? She imagined she looked like some stunned whale washed onto
an unknown shore. On the flight over, she'd asked for the window
seat. She'd let the ticket agent imagine it was so she could see Kabul
on approach. The real reason was less logical. Sitting by the window
gave her the false sense that she could escape if needed, if this whole
venture turned out to be as ridiculous as Jimmy had warned. Now it
became suddenly clear: there was no escaping. There never had been,
not since Jimmy had come home. She'd flown to Kabul in some unacknowledged attempt to bargain with God, or maybe fate, since her
sense of God had become murky: in return for her work here, please,
Whoever, give her son his legs back, so he could lift her up and twirl
her around again, or take a hike, or press pedal to metal in his truck.
Or if that was too much for a simple, sinful woman to ask, at least
please give Jimmy back his spirit.

It was unrealistic and ill-conceived; she recognized that. Never had she been more out of place in her life. But before she could fall into a raging panic in full view of dark-eyed, turbaned men and silent women suffocated in cloth, an officer in an American military uniform strode directly toward her.

"Mrs. Wilkens?"

Thank God for her boy; he'd arranged this, even from bed, even though he disapproved. Mandy felt her eyes well up. Once she'd been the last to cry; often now she was the first. Silently, sternly, she warned her tears to stay put.

"Yes, sir," she said. "That's me."

The officer introduced himself as Corporal Holder. "Welcome," he said. "How much luggage do you have?" She identified one piece after another after another—more, with the medical supplies, than Corporal Holder might have expected, but he showed no surprise as, with fluid movements, he loaded the suitcases and boxes onto a cart. "This way, ma'am," he said, soothingly direct and familiar.

Outside the terminal, Mandy felt dust settle on her skin almost immediately. Holder led the way past a paved expanse to a graveled lot, chatting as they walked. "We're parked all the way over here— sorry. They don't allow you to get too close. How was your flight? You must be tired. I've brought some waters in case you're thirsty. They're in the vehicle. Here we are. And this is PFC Mendez."

Shifting her purse to one side, Mandy managed a handshake with the private. With Holder in the front passenger seat, Mendez at the wheel, and Mandy in the back, they pulled away from the airport.

Afghanistan felt immediately more chaotic than it had in the terminal, which moments earlier Mandy would have said was impossible. Cars hurtled toward one another on what could only loosely be called opposite sides of the road. Horns honked uselessly. Mendez swerved right and then left, careening past trucks, bicycles, men pulling large wooden carts, women in burqas like imploring blue ghosts at the roadside, and finally a legless beggar planted in the middle of the road, empty hands extended before him, undaunted as cars shot by close enough for him to lick if he tried. As they passed him, Mandy sucked in her breath.

Holder turned to look at her and seemed to read her thoughts, even those she couldn't form into words. "Jimmy showed me a couple photos once," he offered. "You look exactly like your pictures, Mrs. Wilkens."

Mandy managed a silent if vacant smile into the rearview mirror. She planned to ask Holder what Jimmy had been like here, and how he'd spent his time when they weren't fighting. But she wanted a more private moment for that conversation.

"So you're from Houston, then?" Mendez spoke over his shoulder.

"Right," Mandy said. "How about you?"

"St. Louis," said Holder.

"New Mexico," answered Mendez. "A little town south of Santa Fe. Watch out, dumbass," he said, addressing a passing vehicle, and then, over his shoulder again, added, "Excuse me, ma'am. They drive crazy here."

"I can see that."

"If you don't mind me asking, ma'am," Mendez said, "but what are you . . . well, what are you doing in Kabul? I mean, Holder here tried to explain, but . . ."

"I'm a nurse preceptor back home," Mandy said.

"Pre-what?"

"I work side by side with nurses that I train in the emergency ward. And we get our share of emergencies, especially on Friday . . ." Mandy trailed off, knowing that an emergency in Houston was nothing like one here. "On Friday and Saturday nights," she finished lamely. "Anyway, I'm here to visit some hospitals, maybe a refugee camp or two. I've brought supplies to hand out—antibiotics, sterile bandages, sutures, that kind of thing. I'll observe. Maybe I can offer some best-practice suggestions on evaluation or triage."

"Pretty brave of you to come here," Mendez said.

"Brave." It hadn't been the word Jimmy had used. Mandy touched the edge of her headscarf as if it were her hair. "I worked for the Peace Corps way back when. I figured if I could do two years then, I could manage a couple weeks now."

"But you're on your own this time."

She shook her head. "I'm working through an NGO that deals with refugees. The in-country director used to be married to a friend of mine. He's connecting me to the people and places."

"And where were you based back in the Peace Corps?"

"Ecuador. I worked in a clinic there."

Mendez drove in silence for a moment. "Forgive me, ma'am," he said, "but I don't imagine Ecuador is much like Afghanistan. Here, we're all just scooping teacups out of the Titanic. I'm probably not supposed to say that kind of shit, you know, morale and all." Mendez twisted the steering wheel to the left, and Mandy lurched into the turn. "I mean, it's great that you still care, that you know this place is part of our own American story by now, with all the blood and treasure spent. Still . . . let's just say I wouldn't want *my* mom here."

"Sorry about my buddy here," Holder said as he socked Mendez's right arm. "He's got too many questions and too many opinions."

"It's all right." Mandy had heard a version of this, only with greater heat, from Jimmy. She'd hoped not to respond to questions like these. She'd hoped to talk only about her desire to help heal others injured by a war that had cost her son his legs. But this Mendez, he could be Jimmy. He even sounded a little like Jimmy used to sound. For reasons she couldn't precisely name, she wanted to give him a fuller picture. "You're right," she said, "I'm not Doctors Without Borders. But I sent a son here to fight. It's the hardest thing I've ever done—you know from your own families. While Jimmy was here, I was living back there, but living differently. I lived with an everyday fear. He returned, thankfully. But he's—you know, he's . . ." She thought about saying *changed*, but she was trying to get at the root of what she felt now, and part of that involved veering away from euphemisms. "He's a double amputee." She paused, find-ing herself surprised again at the ugliness of this phrase. "So it's also personal. I decided to try . . . maybe to understand things better in the end. There have to be Afghan mothers here who feel like I do. I'd like to meet them."

A car honked its horn as it passed them, and Mendez cursed under his breath. "Yeah, well, good luck with your work," he said. "Hell, it's as likely to win hearts and minds as anything else we do out here."

"Jimmy was a good soldier," Holder said after a moment. He turned to Mandy. "So how is he, really?"

This was too complex a question to answer in this hurtling car, in front of strangers. What could she say? That loud noises frighten him and he seems to have forgotten how to laugh? That he says Afghanistan left him forever half a man, and that some nights he grows so dark it scares her, and then he drinks himself into oblivion? That sometimes she feels like she's just waiting for the day he'll give up altogether and become a delayed, unacknowledged fatality of this war, possibly taking her down with him?

She looked out the window, aware of the awkward fall of silence. "He's alive," she said. "In the end, I guess we're lucky."

"Damn straight," Mendez said. Then, mercifully, he turned on the radio, and Arabic-sounding music flooded the car, making Mandy think of young women dancing in gauze dresses. She gazed out the window, remembering when she herself had been a young woman with clingy dresses and shapely legs and an easy stride, a woman who'd not yet cleaned blood off a wound or leaned over a terminal patient or had a baby ripen in her belly.

She rested a hand on her chest, feeling the air move inside her. Something was badly broken in there, she knew. But maybe—and this was the secret hope she'd carried with her from Texas to Dubai and over the yawning stretch of Afghanistan—maybe she'd heal herself in their hospitals, by a taste of the country that had chewed up her son and then spit him back. Maybe, if God existed, if he were truly great, they'd all be healed.

Todd

t he argument had tumbled forward for almost twenty minutes now and had already begun circling back; Todd was ready for ice cream. To a casual observer, the debate might seem one-sided; after all, Amin did all the talking. But Todd had a knack for disagreeing without speaking. His was the art of those too cautious or too isolated to engage in frank exchanges. He'd refined it over years of working far from home, challenging himself to seek persuasion through patience and through words used like pinches of pepper in a delicate dish.

"This isn't our work," Amin said. "I don't trust Zarlasht; her aim is to manipulate," and then, with greater heat, "It's dangerous to involve yourself in a dispute of this sort, Mr. Todd—I feel a responsibility to make sure you understand this," and finally, "It's outside our sphere of responsibility, anyway. We must concentrate on working for refugees."

Todd smiled or grimaced now and then, nodded in a way that indicated nothing more than thoughtfulness, and occasionally glanced out the window. Though his vision was curtailed by the ten-foot-high whitewashed security wall that encased the compound, he knew that just beyond it lay the chaotic life of Kabul streets, where women in burqas clutched kohl-eyed babies and begged at stoplights and men pushing wheelbarrows loaded with bruised fruit swayed between cars with audacity, where underfed children scattered and regrouped to sell pieces of rusted metal intended for purposes Todd could never discern, where traffic lights and lane markings were thought to be for sissies and safe travel was achieved only through great boldness and luck. He longed for it. He longed especially now, stuck in a room of intellectual—and ultimately, he feared, irresolvable—discord.

Finally, blessedly, Amin paused for breath.

"Shall I get us some *sheer yakh*?" Todd asked.

"Why not simply have told her to return on Thursday instead of Wednesday?" Amin said, using what surely had to be the last of his arguing energy. "Then I could have said you were called out of town on an emergency. That might have discouraged her—or at least would have given me time to look into her claims, her family." Todd's travel plans were always secret; Amin, his closest Kabul colleague— no, friend—was the only person here who knew that early Thursday, just before *fajr* prayers, Todd would depart for Islamabad. By Thursday evening, he would be waist-deep in issues involving refugees in Pakistan, and Zarlasht would have been turned away at the gate. After four weeks in Pakistan, Todd would return for one more month in Kabul, his last. Then back to New York, and to Clarissa, for good, though Amin hadn't yet been told that, and of course that involved challenges of its own. Challenges not to be considered now; Todd always said his doctors insisted that, for his continued good health, he ignore all problems outside his current time zone.

"Because, Amin, we cannot simply dismiss this as beyond our mandate." Todd kept his voice neutral in contrast to Amin's heat. "You tell me the villagers are turning to the Taliban for justice. Well, Zarlasht is turning to us. If we do nothing, we are by default supporting the Taliban."

"How many years do I know you now, Mr. Todd? Long enough for me to say that you are still too trusting, and my words are not a—how do you say?—a compliment. You—"

But Todd held up his hand, cutting Amin off. "Wait, my friend. First . . ." He reached to a tray on a table in the corner, lifted two small glass bowls, and raised his eyebrows in a question.

Amin let out an exasperated breath. "Too late for ice cream," he said.

"Oh, Amin, we haven't reached the end of the world yet. And even then—"

"Your cook told me to strictly forbid you from eating ice cream after 3 p.m. because otherwise, you won't eat her dinners."

"Yes," Todd agreed. "Shogofa will not be happy with me. But there's nothing for it; *sheer yakh* it must be. It will clear our brains. Remember, we have the late meeting with the American nurse, Mandy Wilkens."

"I didn't forget," Amin said. "But Mr. Todd, do you really want ice cream, or just to escape my reasonable words?"

"The ice cream. Okay, *mostly* the ice cream." Todd, mock-somber, laid his palm on his chest. "I swear."

Amin shook his head in resignation. "One scoop," he said. "Only one."

Todd grinned as he headed out the office door and down the steps to the main entrance, where he slipped his shoes on. He nodded to his driver, Farzad, smoking by the car. *"Salaam alekum,"* he said to Mustafa, the building guard, who emerged from a small room next to the metal gates. Todd raised the ice-cream cups as if they were admission tickets, which, in a way, they were.

Todd was required to travel everywhere by reinforced car with tinted windows: to refugee camps, government offices, the UN compound, the rare meal out, even the five blocks to the guesthouse where he slept. He sat in the back, with Farzad driving and Jawwid in the front passenger seat toting an AK-47. Those who came to Todd's office were not allowed through the gate unless they'd made a prior appointment and even then were thoroughly checked by his guards. "Your safety is a matter of our honor," Amin had explained. Todd understood, but this meant that everything in his Kabul environment was tightly controlled, which was not the way he functioned best. To do his job well, he needed to walk down narrow, dusty roads as they descended into yet unknown villages and to visit the overfilled refugee camps. In fact, he came to life visiting homes fashioned of war rubble and roofed with UN-provided tarps, eating unimaginable food he hoped would not make him ill, witnessing the tremendous grace and imagination of the vulnerable. He loved the unexpected adventure of every day spent in the field. He got to do little enough of it as regional director, given all the desk work combined with safety concerns. And he'd soon be giving up even that.

But today he still had the ice-cream run.

Over the five and a half years that he'd been coming to this office, Todd had posited and reposited compromises to ease the restraints he faced in the name of security. At last his grumblings had evolved into a discussion: Todd, Amin, Farzad and Jawwid sitting on floor mats, drinking *chai*, Todd offering that both his job and his personal needs required more relaxed access to Kabul, at least occasionally, and the Afghan men talking among themselves at a speed that defied his limited Pashto. Finally, a little over a year ago, they had reluctantly agreed to let him walk the block and a half from the office to the ice-cream stand, no Jawwid at his side, no Farzad following in the car. But, equally firmly, nowhere else. So this had become his nearly daily outing, the only moments when he could imagine himself free in this teeming ancient city of conflict and joy and loss that enchanted him.

"How are you, Mr. Todd Barbery?" Mustafa asked in English as he opened the gate, making the second word sound elongated. Mustafa was the only Afghan who insisted on calling Todd by first and last name.

"Teh kha, manana," Todd responded, as was their practice. One in English, the other in Pashto, and sometimes they expanded their respective vocabularies in a fleeting language lesson. At the moment, though, Todd desired no further words. He kept moving, waved good-bye, and heard the gate clang shut behind him. The sound of freedom.

The air was golden, which really meant full of dust, but Todd chose to see it in more romantic terms. He walked slowly, lingering, stretching his leash to its ends. He admired the energy of this mountain-ringed city—founded, it was said, by Cain and Abel, visited by Genghis Khan, loved by Babur, beaten down over and over, but with a core of perseverance and unlikely optimism. He found the faces of its people beautiful, a human mosaic of endurance creased with dark but resilient humor. These were qualities he valued; Afghanistan had found its way into his blood. The ice-cream run was the most dependably enjoyable part of his Kabul day. He was grateful for the break from those who both helped him in uncountable ways and made him feel chained. And Afghan ice cream, seasoned with rosewater and cardamom and topped with grated pistachios, was a small miracle in a land that desperately needed miracles.

The boy Churagh ran to Todd, waving his newspapers. "How are you?" he said in over-enunciated English. Churagh had identified Todd as a soft touch; he bought a paper and gave the boy's arm a friendly squeeze. Sometimes they chatted and Todd bought a second newspaper. Today Churagh seemed to sense Todd's preoccupation; he followed but kept a distance. Though he wouldn't admit it to Amin, Todd was having trouble shaking the unease brought on by the conflict between his desire to help Zarlasht somehow and the strength of Amin's arguments. He wanted to play Zarlasht's visit over in his mind without Amin's voice in his ears.

This had been Zarlasht's third visit to Todd's office—too many for simple courtesy calls. Mostly, he was the one who called on government officials, and the visitors he did have at the Kabul office were usually NGO representatives, not hospital administrators like Zarlasht, so he'd been vaguely uneasy about what she might want from him. When she'd arrived, she had not been shown to the meeting room full of cushions; instead, she'd sat on a chair in front of his desk. Amin stood in the corner so that Zarlasht would not suffer any harm to her reputation by being alone with a Western man. She wore, as always, a headscarf, no burqa. He guessed she was about forty years old, although he'd found that the stress and want of their lives took a toll on Afghans, and he knew she could easily be a decade younger.

The first time she visited, Zarlasht chatted without making any specific request; she said she'd heard good things about him and wanted to meet, since she worked as an administrator in Maiwand Hospital and often dealt with refugees. The next time, she told a story about her grandfather, a story of captivity and separation, her grandfather taken away by the Soviets and she a child, so scared, hanging on to his robe, chanting, "Please don't go, don't go, Granddad."

"Not to worry, my dear," the grandfather had said, a soldier flanking him on each side.

"Where are you going?"

"Only out to buy you a television set," the grandfather said, a story so improbable only a child would believe it. "I'll come back with it soon."

"When?"

"An hour. Two at most. Before dark, surely."

So she released her hold on him. And did not see him again for two and a half years—infinity in the life of a child—until he appeared one afternoon in the home she shared with her mother and grandmother. Sitting at the table, her grandfather smiled and raised his hand in greeting. But she didn't recognize the frail stranger. "Who is this man? Why is he here? What does he want?" she asked her grandmother, and at that, his smile slid away and he began to weep. They'd pulled out his nails in prison, roots and all, so he had only the soft ends of his fingers, and he'd received electric-shock torture so many times it had left a hole in his tongue. He couldn't eat, couldn't bear food in his damaged mouth, so he was fed intravenously until his death, less than two years later.

Political discord in this land had always been marked by blood and pain. The stories were unending, shocking the first time, sad but predictable after that. Still, Todd had been moved not only by her story but by the simple way in which she told it, without melodrama or any apparent attention to its effect on him. On the way out the door, almost as an afterthought, Zarlasht had mentioned a cousin who was being beaten by her husband.

That cousin was the focus of her visit today.

"Things are worsening for her," Zarlasht said, starting in even before the cup of *chai* arrived. "She can stand that her husband beats her, but she cannot stand the beating of her only daughter. Last week he poured boiling oil on the girl's legs. They will be scarred. We are lucky it was not her face."

"I'm so sorry."

"My cousin is determined to stop him," she said.

"She is brave."

Zarlasht turned her head away as she nodded. "My cousin's father went to the elders," she said, gazing as if at someone no one else could see. "He asked that a *jirga* be held to hear her complaints against her husband. They agreed at first, but now her husband has gone to them and sought their support, and they are threatening to cancel the hearing and instead punish her for speaking against her husband."

"Can't her father help?"

"He is not as powerful as her husband," Zarlasht said. "It is whispered that the *jirga* wants to stone her for defying her husband and encouraging other women to do the same. Also as a show of strength, so the foreign occupiers—forgive me, but this is how they speak— can see that *sharia* holds sway less than seventy kilometers from Kabul. It's not her own life that she considers. She doesn't want her daughter left alone with a father who views her as an object. In this case, the girl will have no future at all."

Zarlasht did not cry during this small speech, but her eyes were tight with an anguish that seemed so personal Todd felt sure she was speaking of herself, not a cousin. His natural impulse was to reach to squeeze her hand, but he knew this would violate all kinds of cultural protocol. He looked out the window for a minute instead, and then turned back. "I'm so sorry about all this, Zarlasht. But why come to me?"

"Because I know your reputation," Zarlasht said. "I think if you summon Haji Mulak, and you mention the name of my . . . my cousin's husband, it might make a difference. Say you want to know about the case of Hamid, his wife and daughter."

Todd smiled. "I fear your confidence in my reach is unrealistic."

"I don't think so. They talk about how you go to see the refugee camps, and how more food and doctor visits follow." Zarlasht paused, then spoke in a slightly softer voice. "And I have nowhere else to go."

That sentence hung in the silent room for a moment, sucking out its air. Todd glanced briefly at Amin, whose eyes carried a clear warning. "Give me a few days," he told Zarlasht. "Let me see if I can help. Come back Wednesday."

"*Tashakor*," she said, putting her right hand to her chest. "*Ma salaam*."

She barely looked at Amin as she left, and no sooner had she walked from the building than Amin began to argue. "This is not your business, Mr. Todd. It is a local affair. To interfere in this matter is not only useless but perilous. She must know this. So I wonder why she comes to you."

Though Amin was a private man, Todd had heard something of his past, enough to reinforce his trust in Amin's political instincts. As a teenager, Amin had waited on Najibullah while the ousted president was held in the UN mission. With the Taliban takeover, he'd fled over the mountains to Pakistan, joining other refugees. Eventually he got a scholarship to be educated in the States, then returned to Afghanistan. He had a wife, three daughters, and a son who lived outside Kabul and whom he saw only at week's end, leaving his brother to look after them day-to-day. Amin believed the best future for Afghanistan lay in an alliance with America, but he also believed Americans were blind to Afghan cultural nuances, failing to understand how telling someone what they wanted to hear had become a survival skill and how quickly and violently apparently seamless alliances could be shattered.

Todd generally followed Amin's advice; in fact, he wasn't sure he'd ever before resisted this insistent an argument. But Amin was all logic and reason, lists of pros and cons, risks to be considered, unlikely gains to be weighed. Todd knew all that; he knew what was allowed here, what wasn't, and still, in these last of his remaining days on the job, he wondered about the advantages of simply speaking out, trying to do the right thing. He knew better than to express that aloud; Amin would invoke cultural differences and surely call him naive besides.

From a half-block away, Todd could see a longer-than-usual line at the ice-cream stand, jammed not with the children who generally gathered there—even Churagh had given up trailing him—but with men, maybe a dozen. Odd; he wondered about it for a moment. Outside the enclosed marketplace, crowds were rare. Fear of suicide bombers always rumbled in the subconscious, and beyond that, of course, a group of any size drew the unwelcome attention of passing troops, whether Afghan or foreign.

He quickly dismissed his worry as paranoia—this was *ice cream* he was talking about—and joined the back of the line. He raised a hand to the two men dressed in long white overshirts and loose pants who dished the ice cream into cups on a table topped with a bright red, plastic sheet. By this time, the vendors knew Todd by sight and generally greeted him with big smiles. Sometimes he ate his ice cream right there in front of the stand, chatting with simple words, pretending for a moment he belonged and could linger casually. Now, though, they were too busy to acknowledge Todd, if they even saw him.

He turned his attention to the bakery next door. In a room not much larger than a closet, three men tossed and patted dough and then submerged it in an open fire-pit to make *bolani* and *nani Afghani*. Sweat beaded their temples. Their bodies moved as if in hypnotic dance.

Something about the scene, though exotic, evoked home. He thought, then, of Clarissa; her name came into his mind, and immediately he felt a tightening in his chest. He thought of her neck, and her long waist. He thought of her voice floating from the bathroom, the door open but she unseen, bent over the sink or patting dry her face, telling him a story from her day. He always found that to be the most intimate of moments—to be with a woman in early evening, lying on a bed, listening to her voice coming from within the bathroom as she brushed or washed away the soil of the hours before. He closed his eyes and rubbed his forehead and saw a fleeting image of his wife. Clari, Clari, Clari.

How had this amazing thing even happened to him, sharing a home again with a wife? He still wasn't sure. He'd been widowed twenty-two years ago, losing Mariana when Ruby was only six. He'd never planned to marry again, throwing all his energy first into being a single parent and then into his work. They'd met at a party. Clarissa was an urban historian teaching at Columbia. Whoever had casually introduced them—he couldn't remember that detail—had noted that she'd recently finished a paper on historic housing patterns in Manhattan. He hadn't been sure what that meant, but he'd immediately liked her smile, so he'd blundered forward, saying he'd noticed from his work with refugees how people arranged their living spaces even among war rubble, when you'd think shelter would be their only concern. A hierarchy developed, he'd gone on. Desirable housing locations arose in ways indiscernible to average outsiders, based on issues such as position relative to the main entrance and the water supply as well as proximity to certain families once considered more powerful. Some tents, he said, were erected a few inches further from their neighbors than others; this sign of status was noted—and accepted—by the camp inhabitants. It all happened without any apparent discussion, so that even when no one had any money worth mentioning, socio-economic groupings occurred.

As he was saying all this, talking almost without breathing just to keep her from walking away, he was really noticing her energy, her way of standing, the look in her eyes, her hair, and again, her smile.

Less than a year later, they married. It felt crazy, unexpected, and right. When they met, he was in the middle of the three-months-in, three-months-out rotations to Kabul and Islamabad. At first she'd been fine with it, but last year she'd offered—as if cupping her words in her hands and holding them out for him to see—that she wanted him to stop. She was careful, so he knew it was still his choice. But he also knew what she thought. It had become too dangerous. The separations were too long; he had a home to return to, and they had a life to build, and too little time.

So he'd agreed to the request she hadn't quite voiced; he was doing his last rotation. He would celebrate his fiftieth birthday at home in three months and then stay there through the next birthday, and the one after that.

And she seemed glad, but she was edgy still, maybe even more so when he'd agreed to quit, thus tacitly acknowledging the dangers. He'd detected it in her voice when they'd spoken a couple of hours ago by phone, as he began his morning, as she headed into sleep.

"There was a bombing in Islamabad a few hours ago," she'd said.

"Yes, I heard."

"Skip going there. Just come directly back."

"I'll be fine."

She made a sound that indicated skepticism. "I feel like a military bride, Todd. And what are we doing still there? Really, at this point?"

"Helping people who need it."

"That sounds so damned sanctimonious," she murmured.

"I'm sorry. But I have to finish up properly. For them. For me."

The line went silent for a moment. "Have they named your replacement yet?" she asked.

"Not yet."

"But they will, yes? You won't offer to stay on for one more rotation?"

"No, Clari. No."

She released a noisy sigh of air into the phone receiver. "Okay, then," she said. And she tried—they both did—to lighten the conversation, to talk about smaller things. But it didn't work; he felt the space gaping between them and knew she did too by her tone when she told him she loved him. He repeated it back, and they said good-bye.

Now he realized he wanted to meet Zarlasht's needs because he *couldn't* meet Clari's. Illogical, of course. But it was as if showing kindness to Zarlasht could make up for hurting his wife, one in exchange for the other. He needed to consider Zarlasht independently. He would try, on the walk back, with his ice cream.

But the line, Todd noticed, did not seem to be moving, though the vendors were bent over their sweet, cold tubs. "Ice cream is popular today," he said to the man in front of him, speaking in Pashto.

The man turned toward Todd. He was about twenty-five years old. He wore a blue-gray turban and a brown vest over his *salwar kameez*, and his eyebrows were unusually thick, like angry storm clouds hovering over his eyes. "It is the best ice cream in Kabul," he said in a way that seemed too serious, so weighted that Todd grinned, thinking for a second he must be kidding.

Then the man turned abruptly away, leaving Todd to stare up at the high, teasing blue of the sky and think about how Afghanistan, even after all these years, had remained just beyond his reach of comprehension. While this concerned him occasionally, it also inspired him and was, in fact, something he loved: the rich, unknowable quality of living here that made his own life feel so much more consequential. A rush of gratitude flooded him, warming his stomach, making him smile faintly. And this was exactly the expression on his face at the moment of the improbable crack of thunder that preceded the dropping of two glass ice-cream cups, and then the silence.

Danil

September 4th

igh clouds, a distant rumble. A shout-out from a storm on the approach tonight, a summer storm pushing its way into the crowded Brooklyn streets from beyond some border, like an audacious illegal immigrant or a country girl thumbing her nose at the pretensions of civilization. Danil had maybe half an hour before it broke, and he planned to use the minutes well. His right arm blurred as he shook the can so energetically it made his whole body bounce. If some half sleeper a few stories above the street in the Albany House II projects were to pause on the way to the toilet, bladder full, eyes bleary, and glance out his apartment window to the empty lot below, Danil would seem an unlikely dancer responding to absent music, a drunk or whack job ripe for the Kingsboro Psychiatric Center. The can's rattling seemed magnified in the night air, resounding off the concrete around him. The corner of Bergen and Albany remained sunk in postmidnight somnolence, the darkness gobbling up noise and movement and regurgitating them as indistinct fragments of dreams. In this space of relative obscurity, he began.

As if in a private ritual of nightly prayer, Danil's holy paint met the sanctified wall. He moved his arm in graceful waves. After several minutes, he lowered the spray can to his side and then touched a corner of the paint with the tip of his left baby finger to test for dryness. He pulled off the paper, refolded it quickly, and extracted the next layer of stencil from where he'd stashed it under a parked car. With painter's tape, he put the new cutout in place, holding his flashlight in his mouth so he could see to line it up properly.

As he worked, he sang "Mr. Tambourine Man," just loud enough to make the back of his mouth vibrate. Dylan had been Danil's quirky brother Piotr's favorite singer, and just a few weeks ago, Danil had heard that song covered by a gutter punk band whose name he couldn't remember in the Rock Star Bar under the Williamsburg Bridge. A dive with a great view of the span over the East River, a neon air-hockey table, and two carved ship figureheads that hung above the liquor shelves, the bar was an odd place peeled off an earlier, rougher time; Danil liked it mainly because of the layers of scrawled tags that covered every inch of the bathroom, which was often where people gathered to talk, smoke, share drugs. And when the band of forgotten name performed, the Dylan song was etched onto the night like a Sunday choir's hymn by a rope of a man with tattoos running up both arms. The singer forwent the harmonica, and his voice was raspier than Dylan's, but it made Danil wish he could call Piotr. And it planted in his brain lyrics perfect for a street artist hoping to be immune to the night.

Danil killed the flashlight, dug in his backpack for the can of white, and silenced himself in concentration. This was the most important coat, the detail layer, full of fine cuts. It would take him a few minutes longer than the others, but it was manageable, assuming no one came strolling down the street. In this neighborhood at this hour, he was less worried about being arrested than being jumped.

As he moved the can back and forth, he felt awake to the blood flowing in his arms, to the white paint as it spewed out, and to the goose-bump quality of the brick wall coated with a thin, patchy layer of cement. This was what it meant to be alive. Near the edges of the paper, he shortened his swing to avoid overspray. His mind was doing double duty, checking the coverage while listening so intently for any unusual street noise that he imagined his ears turned inside out. He glanced over his shoulder and then turned back to the wall, conscious of the cool night air sailing over his arms.

Danil was thirty-one, too old for vandalism, maybe too old for all this shit, even in the name of protest art. But nothing beat the feeling he got when painting the street. Only then did he feel light, an organic part of the world around him, yet disconnected from the dark thoughts of Piotr or his mother. Piotr, younger and so much more talented than Danil, had been drawn to bugs and small creatures, a collector of butterfly wings and ladybug shells, and such an easy target for grade school thugs. Where the older brother was mild, the younger veered all the way to timid, and bullies sensed this. "It's your job to look after him," their mother used to tell Danil. "You are four years older, and so much stronger, and not so dreamy. You've got to take care of him when I'm not there."

And he had, for years. Though he was thin and quiet, Danil didn't mind using his fists against anyone who tried to torment his brother. When they were both in high school, Piotr started calling him a "golden toad," a reference picked up from one of the nature magazines he loved. He said he meant that Danil appeared gentle but could turn aggressor when needed. Danil always laughed and said anyone who talked about golden toads and ladybug elytras and brush-footed butterflies clearly needed a protector. Still, somehow it was mild Piotr who had been persuaded after a single year at college to go help fight a war, some damn unfathomable idealism kicking in. And somehow it was Danil who found that fight foolish.

These days their mother, who ran her used bookstore at the edge of Cleveland, Ohio, had grown thick with refusal, dodging the truth about Piotr and writing long letters to Danil. One of the last ones he'd read included a snapshot, tattered at the lower left corner. "A photo of me and my two boys. Can you tell me why . . ." When Danil and his mother were together, her confusion deepened and their sorrows seemed to multiply. When they were together, they could neither deny Piotr's absence nor ignore the distance left between them by his death. So Danil never answered the letters, never called home anymore.

Instead, he stenciled on crumbling brick walls of deserted buildings, on rusting metal factory doors, and once on the side of a van abandoned in an empty lot. While he was working on the sketches, cutting the stencils, he thought about Piotr. He remembered some things, he realized others about his brother. But while he was actually doing the work in the middle of some half-blind night, the anguish finally settled. There was no past, no future to concern him, only here and now, and him alive, the sound of paint misting from an upright can.

When he finished with the white, he waited again, testing for dryness. Then he quickly removed the paper and backed up next to an abandoned car seat. He checked the street to his right and left—still empty—before turning on his flashlight.

Sometimes he practiced on one wall in his run-down studio apartment. He'd tried out this stencil there, painting over the remnants of other projects, a trial run to make sure the layers came together as he'd hoped. He'd felt fine enough about the results. But the outcome always looked different on location. When he planned it right, the environment—fading tags on marred cement walls, straggly weeds fringing tall buildings—multiplied the meaning of the image. Now, something nearing satisfaction swept through Danil's body, not pride exactly but a kind of certainty that this work was deeply moral. Ephemeral art, echoing ephemeral life, and randomly finding its temporary partners.

He thought of people seeing the piece in the morning as they headed into the bodega on the corner or the high school across the street. He imagined a couple of kids sitting on the grounded bench seat, facing the wall, studying his work, really seeing it: a life-sized woman with a serious expression, dancing on top of an oversized clenched fist, and wearing a black dress with red teardrops falling from the hem.

His brother's body had arrived home with a medal attached, but Piotr was not a war hero, not in any traditional sense. Instead, he'd become a victim of a creative effort to rewrite the present. To sanitize it. So Danil had become a Reminderer; he considered it his unpaid, untitled job. *Dear passerby, plugged into your smart phone, lost in one form of oblivion or another: if you focus on a middle distance, you will remember. Ravenous war is upon us still.*

He was not yet finished. One more plastic piece taped on the wall.

One more can of paint, a pale yellow. On the black of the dress, he painted the flag's stars, meant for irony. And beneath the stencil of the coffin, four capital letters, about five inches tall, the sole bit of obvious, if destructible, ownership he allowed himself. IMOP. His tag.

He stepped back to examine the piece again and felt his shoulders drop slightly in relaxation. It was as he'd hoped; it was good. For tonight, there would be no nightmares to jar him awake, no shout climbing from his throat. For tonight, sleep would be restorative enough, fueled by this moment, his toe-dip into a well of fulfillment, an emotion surely as transient as street art itself, yet nonetheless valuable. Here lay the lesson for him, he thought, in both what had happened to his brother and the work he left on the street. In everything, temporary is inevitable; the wise accept it as enough.

Clarissa

September 4th

I n the narrow strand of space between the first piece of information and all the rest, thoughts rushed through Clarissa that could not be said aloud, not then, probably not ever. They came like the violent Nor'easters she'd known as a child in Maine, appearing without warning as she'd disconnected the phone for the third time in quick succession.

How could he have let this happen?

The initial call came from a reporter, and Clarissa hung up mid-sentence, telling herself there'd been a mistake.

He tricked me. Tricked me into trusting him, despite me knowing that life is delicate beyond belief and humans are flimsy, even those who seem invincible.

The second call came from Bill Snyder, who opened by barely speaking at all, as if to prolong her last moments of unknowing, and then began carefully, each word padded by pauses, each phrase couched in ambiguity. She hung up on him also, but with less confidence.

Everything one counts on can vanish in a second; I'd understood that since childhood. A new narration wiping out personal history without a whisper of remorse. So why had I let myself willfully block out this transiency, fall in love, remake the boundaries of my life, and then redefine what it meant to trust the world?

The final call came from a baldly definitive FBI agent, speaking in a clipped but almost tender tone as she thought in stunned amazement, "The FBI; how odd is this?" She had no memory of hanging up on him, only of noticing at one point that she no longer pressed the receiver to her ear.

Somehow, I'd secretly relied on the conviction that he would stay safe. He had a plan and I'd become a late believer in the power of planning. I trusted our future as much as the fact that ice was cold and fires were hot and letters arranged on a page would remain readable. That much trust was too much.

The mind is a labyrinth capable of holding at once the ocean, the sky, and everything in between; of carrying on four simultaneous conversations, most of them internal; of dismissing one memory even as it accesses another in detail and creates a third.

"At least he was doing what he loved." Didn't people in situations like this say that? Wasn't that a ridiculous thing to say?

These thoughts pushed their way up from the floor of her mind, edging aside other, more critical judgments and understandings and misunderstandings.

humans are delicate so keep it safe humans are impermanent so take the risks humans are transient so soak in the details humans are temporary so think big humans are breakable so be diligent humans are ephemeral so be carefree humans are fragile so

Thoughts came that she would register unconsciously and quickly forget but would recall—some of them, at least—much later, in her revised world, as pieces of her future settled into new patterns of fleetingness.

What do we do now? What do I do now?

Mandy

mandy understood immediately how secure this guest-house was. Even though she was a harmless-looking middle-aged woman who arrived with two uniformed American soldiers, the guard would not let her in until he'd summoned Hammon and gotten his okay.

Hammon was six foot three with short hair, black leather boots, an easy walk, and biceps three times the size of hers. He pushed back his sunglasses so she could see his eyes and, though she'd never met him before, greeted her warmly. "Mrs. Wilkens, come in," he said, waving an offhanded good-bye to the soldiers as he revealed a strong British accent. "Let me show you to your room. Rumi—he's our cook—should have dinner ready soon. Rumi's a pro; you can safely eat even salad inside this compound. He grows his own lettuce right here and washes it with our water."

Jimmy had met Hammon during some kind of special military training that he'd never fully explained. He did say Hammon had taken a liking to him and would turn up from time to time on Jimmy's base. Hammon was a former SAS soldier who now worked as a private security guard in Afghanistan—a top one, Jimmy had said, the kind who destroys and replaces his cell phone every week, and knows the underground entrances to government offices, and takes on assignments too top secret to ever be mentioned. Jimmy had said hotels for internationals had become crime magnets, and staying at Hammon's guesthouse was the safest thing Mandy could do, if she insisted on going to Kabul.

Hammon led her to the second floor of what seemed to be the main building. "Here you are," he said, pushing open the door to a small corner room. "Not gorgeous, but it's clean." The room held a built-in closet, a desk, and a bed next to the window. The paint on the walls was gently peeling, the ceiling stained. Mandy tugged open the heavy curtains and glanced out. The high security walls, topped with barbed wire, enclosed a courtyard dotted with rose plants struggling unsuccessfully to achieve a jaunty air. At least the dust combined with the day's light gave everything a burnt -orange wash, which Mandy found mildly comforting.

Hammon stepped to the desk and used his foot to tap a bottom board. It hinged open to reveal two hidden drawers. "This is a good place to leave your passport—just carry a photocopy. You can also stash any extra cash, jewelry, whatever," he said. "And over here—" He went to a landscape painting and pulled the frame away from the wall to reveal a small crawl space, "this is where you hide if you ever need to. It closes from inside. It's dark, but there's enough air for eight hours."

"I've entered another world," Mandy said. "We don't have anything like this back home."

Hammon smiled. "I doubt you'll need it. But it would be foolhardy not to show you." Then he turned suddenly serious. "You're pretty safe within these walls, but we're right in the center of things, and even just outside our gate—let alone in a hospital or refugee camp—you can become a target of opportunity. People here are poor. They spot a foreigner, make a phone call, and get a payoff. That's all it takes. So don't forget it." He paused. "Sorry. Don't mean to lecture."

"It's okay. I've already heard it all from Jimmy."

Hammon shook his head. "Tough break, Jimmy. He's that unusual combination of a real gentleman with a strong street sense, at least for Afghanistan. He's among the best I've ever seen."

Others, Mandy thought, saw things in Jimmy that she never had.

"You know I've offered him a job when he gets back on his feet," Hammon continued.

No, Mandy hadn't known, and the phrase "back on his feet" made her cringe. But she nodded vaguely. "In Afghanistan?"

"I don't know if he'll want to come back, but he'd be good at it. How's he doing?"

Why did she always stumble over this question? Because she felt she was supposed to say fine, and there was progress, and all that. She was supposed to be grateful her son had made it home, and forget how. "You know how it is," Mandy said. "He's okay."

Hammon nodded, hesitated, and Mandy had the sense he was about to tell her something, maybe something important. But then the guard appeared, spoke to Hammon in Pashto, and handed over a note. Hammon held it out to her.

"A driver just stopped by and left this for you," he said.

It was a single page, folded three times. She opened it carefully.

"Dear Mrs. Wilkens. I am very sorry that it is my duty to inform you Mr. Todd Barbery has been taken from the street by gunmen. I will do everything I can to act on Mr. Todd's behalf in his absence, which I trust will not be long. I cannot meet you today, but tomorrow, please call me at this phone number. 700 201136. Very Best, Amin."

Mandy stared at the words, trying to absorb them. *Todd, kidnapped?* It had been more than a decade since she'd seen him, but they'd been friends of sorts in their youth. Todd had married one of Mandy's closest friends, Mariana, who'd died young. *Todd, kidnapped?* He had long experience in this part of the world, Mandy knew. If he didn't know his way around the dangers here, no outsider did.

"What is it?" Hammon asked.

She handed him back the note and sank down on the edge of the bed.

Hammon read it in one glance and refolded it carefully. "You know, you can turn around right now. If your contact is unavailable, one of the next flights out is an option."

Mandy hesitated only a beat before shaking her head. "No. No, it's not." She took a deep breath. "I came all this way. I'm not leaving at the first sign of trouble. Jimmy didn't. You don't."

"Jimmy said you were pretty determined."

"I bet 'determined' isn't the word he used."

Hammon grinned. "Can I keep this note for a little bit? Before you go anywhere, I want to check out this Amin person."

"Of course."

"Take some rest, Mrs. Wilkens. Rumi should have dinner soon. It's downstairs. He rings a bell, and we all throng in." Hammon left, closing the door behind him.

Mandy lay back on the bed, dropping her head against a pillow that felt as if it were filled with rice. She closed her eyes. She wouldn't tell Jimmy about the kidnapping, she decided. And at dinner, she'd ask Hammon to keep quiet about it as well if he should talk to her son. In the distance, she heard the start of the hypnotic call to prayer. She realized that the jet lag, the travel, and the news about Todd had left her feeling deeply tired and yet too buzzed to nap. She would unpack her clothes in the quiet before dinner. It would be a symbolic commitment to her decision to stay, no matter what. So she rose, tugged open a zipper on her suitcase, and began settling into the thick-walled room in the heart of a dusty foreign city.

Clarissa

September 4th

Clarissa pushed her way outside to stand on the front stoop; her apartment felt confining. She couldn't bear to be waiting from *in there* for whatever would happen next *out here*. Her cheeks were slapped by a brilliant, raw morning, too bright and too cold for September, a morning already being spliced into haiku-like moments that would never, no matter how she tried, coalesce into a whole.

The air had an odd consistency, like Jell-O, and for several minutes she felt as though she had to concentrate on eating the sky in large, unappetizing gulps in order to stay alive. In front of a house half a block away, a narrow stretch of a man stood sweeping the sidewalk with a stitch-straw broom, making a scratching sound against the pavement as he gathered leaves into a pile. It was a hopeful act, wasn't it? A belief in the future, in the order of things. She wanted to catch his eyes, maybe to smile or wave, but the bill of a blue cap hid his face and he didn't look up.

Then someone called her name, as a question. "Clarissa?" And there was Bill Snyder, hugging her, his cheek pressing hers for too long, as if it were a sponge absorbing moisture, his fleshy, presumptuous hands swallowing hers, pulling her back inside, and though she tried to resist, to explain that she didn't want to be indoors, he spoke over her: what they knew, what they didn't know, how concerned-hopeful-involved-sorry he was.

And then a blurring, so that events did not stand out as separate. Ruby was suddenly there, less stiff than usual, more vulnerable, the situation bringing into sharp relief that they were family now, something the two of them had silently conspired to ignore. Ruby was with her partner, Angie, and they were quickly followed by Clarissa's brother, Mikey—painful to see his face so blanched, like a visual of her own shock, but thank God for his presence. How had they all found out? Maybe Clarissa had called them? She had no memory of this. Maybe it had been the FBI?

Mikey was speaking, but the words were impossible to discern. Once pronounced, they seemed to dissipate like the exotic, brief scent of Casablanca lilies, the flowers she and Todd had chosen for their wedding in Montauk. Her wedding day. She hurried away from that memory, calling to it over her shoulder, *Not now, not now*, distracting herself by watching the movement of Mikey's lips: tiny, discordant waves that rose and fell cautiously as if he didn't want to open his mouth too wide. Which tight, tense words were managing to escape? Clarissa wondered. Which full ones were being trapped within? "Fabulous," perhaps, or "mandatory"? Words that might apply to Todd, if only they could slip past constricted lips.

Todd. Let them talk around her; Clarissa would concentrate on Todd. Maybe he would just run away from his captors. Maybe he would call and say, "I'm free. Coming home." Maybe even this morning. But from where, from whom would he escape? Was he bound? Was he blindfolded? In a tiny room, the trunk of a car, behind some rocks on a mountainside? As if it might help her find answers, Clarissa checked her iPhone for the weather in Kabul. Sixty-nine degrees and sunny, with an expected high of 84. So at least he wasn't cold. If he was still in Kabul, that is. And that led to other questions, but it was hard to focus on them in the midst of the voices talking around her, to her, over her, a cocoon of voices.

The phone rang, jarring, and Clarissa grabbed the receiver in order to silence it, wishing she could silence everyone around her so easily and claim for herself a moment to think. "Ms. Montague," said a man's voice. "Hi. My name is . . ." Wordlessly, she passed the phone to Mikey. He spoke loudly, waving one arm for emphasis. Again, his words didn't stick with her. And then he hung up.

And now Ruby was next to Clarissa, rubbing her eyes and wiping her nose with a knotted fist, suddenly a bereft child instead of the tough twenty-eight-year-old Clarissa had gotten to know. Ironically, she identified more closely with this side of Ruby. She put an arm around the younger woman, who seemed to be trying to contain herself, and failing. She was rocking in a way Clarissa understood she couldn't control. Clarissa embraced her more tightly, but it was like trying to hold back a breaking wave. Angie, looking miserable, rose to get Ruby a glass of water.

"Those bastards," Ruby said in a voice raw as a skinned knee, a voice that seemed to carry its own echo.

"Let's stay optimistic," Bill Snyder said. "Let's hear what the FBI has to say when they get here."

So Bill was still here, Clarissa thought.

"That's right. Let's wait," Angie said as the doorbell rang over her voice. "Want me to get it?"

Clarissa shook her head. "I'll get it." But she waited, arm still around Todd's daughter, until she felt Ruby gather herself. Then she rose and opened the door to a couple at her threshold. They didn't look like FBI agents. The woman wore dress pants and a suit jacket and carried a large leather purse, but the man was wearing jeans and a long-sleeved T-shirt. They looked about thirty, only a couple of years older than Ruby. Weren't FBI agents supposed to be large and pale and middle-aged? Weren't those things job requisites?

"Clarissa Montague?" the man asked.

"Yes."

"I'm Jack. This is Sandy."

And now the informality of first names. Something else she didn't expect from the FBI, not that she'd ever had any expectations about FBI agents in her home. "Okay," she said, but her legs responded silently: *Not okay*. They were rooted in place. The presence of these two at her doorstep made everything too real.

Jack extracted his ID from his back pocket. "You were expecting us, yes?"

No, I wasn't expecting you. Not you, nor any of this.

She nodded and turned. They followed her into her kitchen.

"This is my brother, Mikey," she said. "And my stepdaughter, Ruby, and her partner, Angie. And my husband's colleague Bill." She paused. "And these are the agents. Jack and Sandy." The barest and most incomplete of introductions had already worn her out. "Do you want something?" she asked. "A cup of tea or . . ."

"No, we're good," Jack said.

Good? They each took a chair. Fortunately, the kitchen table was large enough to seat eight. Todd had considered it overkill, but Clarissa loved a big kitchen table as much as she loved the city, though they seemed like opposing impulses. The city was layer after endless layer of life, an impossible promise of infinity, while the kitchen table was more personal, inclusive and nurturing.

This was supposed to be the nurturing stage of her life.

A thick silence waiting to be born into something darker swallowed the room. At last, Jack spoke. "I'm sorry about the circumstances that bring us here."

That stilted sentence seemed to prompt Sandy into action; she opened her purse and pulled out a notebook. "When is the last time you had contact with your husband?" she asked.

"Contact? I—" Clarissa cleared her throat. "I already answered a lot of questions on the phone."

"I'm sorry. We need this in person."

Clarissa inhaled. "We spoke on the phone last night. It was about 10 p.m. my time. It was morning of the next day in Kabul. I guess it must have been a few hours before . . ." She broke off, unable to put it into words.

"What did you talk about?"

It was not about, it was around. We talked around an argument about safety, and our future.

"Just small talk," Clarissa said.

"Can you remember anything specific? Anything at all might be helpful. For example, did he mention anything unusual, or any planned outings or meetings?"

God, what had he said that she'd be willing to share with these strangers sitting in her home wanting to sift through her underwear drawer? She struggled to remember precisely. "An Afghan woman was coming to see him in the office. He wasn't sure what she wanted. He also was to meet some woman from Texas who wanted to visit a refugee camp. And he mentioned his assistant, Amin. He's very close to Amin. That's it."

"Do you need Amin's contact info?" Bill Snyder asked, and then Clarissa's attention wandered as he provided it and Agent Sandy wrote.

"What about you?" Jack asked Ruby after several minutes

"I haven't spoken to him in maybe two weeks." Ruby's voice sounded shaky. "At least not directly."

"Directly?" Jack made an open-handed gesture that indicated puzzlement.

"We're playing an online chess game," Ruby explained. "He makes a move in the evening his time, and I make a move in the evening my time. He made the last move, about four days ago. I . . ." Ruby began to choke up, restrained herself with effort. "It was my turn next."

"Did he mention anything in particular to you? Anyone he was meeting, or anything going on in his life?"

"We really only talked about chess," Ruby said. "We talk about light things when he is overseas. When he's home, that's when he tells me more serious stories."

"Did he ever bring up being threatened in any way?" Jack asked, his tone casual.

"Not really."

"He knew—*knows* that part of the world is not the safest," Clarissa said. "But he always said he felt well protected. And he was getting ready to quit. Is going to quit. He's going to work from New York after this rotation." She glanced toward Bill Snyder, expecting him to nod in acquiescence, but his face remained expressionless, noncommittal, and she fleetingly wondered if he'd tried to talk Todd out of leaving the fieldwork. "You know, Todd worked on *behalf* of Afghans," Clarissa said. "Do his kidnappers get that?"

"Simply being a foreigner—"

"I know. I know, of course," Clarissa interrupted Jack.

"This is a business," Jack continued. "He's an American, and he was accessible. A target of opportunity. It's that simple."

"What was he doing?" Clarissa turned to Bill Snyder. "I mean, when they . . ."

Bill Snyder shrugged. "Getting ice cream, Amin says."

"Christ," Clarissa said.

The kitchen fell silent for a moment. "And you?" Sandy asked Mikey.

Mikey shrugged. "Clari's my only sibling. My only family, really. We're close," he said. "But I wouldn't know about Todd's life day to day, beyond what Clari might mention."

Sandy turned to Angie. "Tell me about your connection to the family."

"Well, Ruby and I, we live together."

"How long have you known each other?"

"I lived with Todd and Ruby for a while when I was a teenager," Angie said

"How long?"

"About a year."

"What were the circumstances?"

Angie shrugged. "Things were not going so great at home. Todd agreed to take me in. He fed me, watched over me, became a surrogate dad. Probably more than he bargained for."

"We understand you work as a psychic," Jack said.

Angie looked as surprised as Clarissa felt. How had they found out so much so quickly? Though she didn't ask the question, Jack seemed to anticipate it. He shrugged in a silent answer.

"I'm an RN," Angie said after a minute. "I work with a hospice. But yes, I do psychic fairs on the side, that kind of thing. That's all."

"So you get premonitions?"

"Sometimes," Angie said hesitantly.

"Can you describe one for us?"

"I hope this is not the primary basis of your investigation," Clarissa said, her voice cool.

"Yeah," Angie said. "I actually don't think this will be helpful."

"They're just trying to think of everything," Ruby said in a soothing way that almost made Clarissa smile. She'd seen this side of Ruby with her father, too: a torrent of emotion almost as if she were a still rebellious teenager and then, at lightning speed, everything under control.

"Okay, well," Angie began, her voice sounding doubtful, "last week there was this guy on the subway platform. It was about ten minutes after 5, and I was headed home from work; he was wearing earphones and dark jeans and swaying to the music on his iPod and he looked like, you know, a regular commuter, a little trance-like, into his own isolated world, but whatever. And suddenly he stared right at me in a piercing way that made me think . . . well, that he was dead. I know it sounds strange, but that's how it felt. And that he wanted me to do something, tell someone . . ."

"Go ahead," Jack encouraged.

"I looked around, and the platform was crowded, and I had no idea who to approach, or what to say if I did, and then my train came, and I looked behind me, and I couldn't see him anymore, you know, like he was lost in the flush of travelers, so I got on the car, and I figured, oh, well, that's it, I must be imagining things."

Sandy had stopped taking notes, and Clarissa agreed with that decision. *Please*, she wanted to shout, *let's get serious here.*

"Yes?" Jack said encouragingly.

"Two mornings later, I took one of those free newspapers they hand out at the subway entrance, I think it was *AM New York*, and I was flipping through it, and there it was. A photo of a man who'd stepped onto the tracks at my station shortly after 5 p.m. *My* man."

"Wow," Sandy said, though she didn't sound particularly impressed.

"She's pretty amazing," Ruby said.

"Have you had any feelings about Ruby's dad?" Jack asked.

"No, no." Angie looked embarrassed. "God, no."

"Now can I ask you a few questions?" Clarissa asked. "Because while all this may serve some purpose that is not occurring to me at this moment, it seems clear what we really need to focus on is what's happening on the ground in Kabul. Who are you talking to? Where do you think my husband is being held, and by whom?"

Jack nodded. "I know it's frustrating at this stage. And though there's a lot we don't know yet, we also aren't fully in the dark. There was, as you know, an explosion on the street where he was standing.

Two people were killed, but we believe the attack was mainly diversionary, and the primary goal was to kidnap your husband. Kidnapping is a big business in Afghanistan. As I'm sure you know."

"So they'd been watching him?" Ruby asked.

Jack shrugged. "What we know is that he was pushed into a white Corolla station wagon and driven away. The Taliban has publicly claimed responsibility; a so-called spokesman contacted Al Jazeera and the AP. So he may be in Taliban hands. Then again, he may not be."

"They would claim responsibility for something they didn't do?" Ruby asked.

"Lots of smoke and mirrors over there," Jack said. "We'll know more soon. Anyway, the first twenty-four to forty-eight hours are the most dangerous."

Clarissa felt light-headed. She tried to think of herself as a rock, solid, connected to the ground.

"You want some water, Clari?" Mikey asked.

"I'm okay. I'm just—I wasn't prepared for this."

"No one's prepared," Jack said. "We've got people all over the world, including some based in hairy places, and everyone ignores what that means until they can't anymore." Clarissa looked at him, trying to read a deeper meaning into his words, but his expression was bland. "I don't want to sugarcoat anything," he said. "You won't end up appreciating that from me. But at least they've already made the initial contact. That's good."

"Good?" someone, maybe Bill Snyder, asked in a voice threaded with sarcasm.

"It's the beginning of an address. They haven't made any demands yet. We think we know where he's being held—I mean, the general area."

"Where?" Ruby asked.

"Southern Afghanistan."

"That *is* general," Mikey said.

"So you don't think he's been moved into Pakistan?" Bill Snyder asked.

"Not at this time," Jack said. "There have been enough of these cases that there's pretty much a pattern. Though, as I've indicated, we aren't completely sure which group has him, and that impacts whether he'll be transferred to another group, and his eventual location, and where they are going to want to hold him for the long term."

"What long term?" Clarissa worked to keep her voice from going shrill.

"Crazy fundamentalists, any way you look at it," Mikey muttered.

"But it matters which ones," Jack said.

Clarissa cleared her throat so she could speak. "What long term?" she repeated.

"We have good connections on the ground. We've learned a lot in the last several years," Jack said. "One thing we need to get squared away. If there is a chance to rescue him, do you want us to go ahead?"

"What do you mean? Of course I want him rescued."

"What he's talking about, Clarissa," said Bill Snyder, "is a military rescue. And he needs your permission because sometimes things go wrong. Sometimes hostages die in rescue attempts."

Again, Clarissa felt dizzy.

"Well, hopefully not," Jack said. "And that's not really what I'm saying, for the record."

"There are those," Bill Snyder continued, "who theorize it is better—safer—to stick with negotiations rather than get impatient and launch a rescue attempt."

Clarissa exchanged a glance with her brother—*How do I process this?*

"What do you advise?" Mikey asked the agents.

"I've spoken to Amin once already this morning," Bill Snyder said quickly. "You've heard Todd talk about him, Clarissa, probably hundreds of times. He has experience and connections, and I have complete trust in him. Besides, he feels extremely responsible toward Todd. He's pursuing leads from his end. I'd like to give him at least a few hours."

"By all means," Jack said. "In fact, it's wise to have locals appear to be leading any negotiations. It keeps the price tag a bit lower. But with American civilians, the U.S. government likes to have the rescue permission lined up, at the ready if it's needed. A two-pronged approach."

"And the decision is Clarissa's?" Ruby asked.

"It's a family decision, of course, but we need the okay from her, yes," Jack said, his voice careful.

Clarissa felt Bill Snyder watching her, holding himself back from saying something more. She felt Ruby's gaze as well. "It's so early; so much is vague. Can't you ask me this when you know more?" she asked. "Then we can discuss it?"

Jack tilted his head to one side thoughtfully. "The men on the ground will certainly tell us the particulars, if there is time. But often, things break quickly. That's why they want your permission on file, as it were."

Clarissa looked at Ruby, then at her hands. She turned toward Jack, examining his face as if she might find something there. His expression was noncommittal. They were all waiting. "I want Todd home," she said. "But I want him home safe."

"We want that, too," Sandy said. "A rescue is only attempted if they feel confident of success on the ground."

"But sometimes in the past, that confidence has been misplaced, hasn't it?" Bill Snyder asked. "Then the hostage can be killed by friendly fire."

. . . humans are delicate so keep it safe humans are impermanent so take the risks . . .

Jack spread open his hands. "It's a war. But our guys succeed more often than they fail."

Bill Snyder shook his head but said nothing. Clarissa took a deep breath. She needed some time. "No military rescue attempt for now." She touched her fingers to her lips as soon as she spoke, almost wishing she could pull back the words, and then lowered her hand to her lap. "Not until we think this through," she said, making her voice more decisive. "Or until we get a little more information about the best way to get Todd home."

Jack looked displeased but managed to shrug. "You're still digesting the information. I understand that. We'll revisit it later. One more thing. In general in these cases, the lower profile, the better." He looked at Ruby, and then glanced at Angie. "It's important to keep it out of the media, and we need your help, too. Don't blog about it or Facebook it, of course. Try not to tell anyone. We're keeping it as quiet as we can, so if a journalist calls, decline comment and refer them to us. The less frenzy, the more time we have to negotiate and to try to pinpoint his whereabouts exactly."

"What else can we do?" Ruby said.

"It may be hard, but try to keep your life as normal as possible. It will be better for you than spending the whole day worrying about what's happening."

"What else?" Ruby repeated.

"As soon as they reach out again, we'll try to push forward the negotiations," Jack said.

"Shouldn't Clarissa be a key part of negotiations?" Bill Snyder asked.

"She'll be intimately involved, of course. But we do have experienced people both in the States and on the ground."

"I appreciate that experience. On the other hand, Todd's family and colleagues will have his interests at heart in the most uncomplicated way," Bill Snyder said. "You guys," he jabbed his chin toward Jack, "have many issues to consider that don't have to do with Todd."

Jack and Bill both turned to Clarissa. Their disagreements clearly carried a subtext Clarissa couldn't follow. She was being asked on the spot to make decisions that could have a direct impact on the outcome of this kidnapping—specifically, on whether or not Todd lived. At the same time, she was being given no tools to help her decide, not even two contacts who agreed on how to proceed. It would be unnerving to speak directly to Todd's kidnappers, she imagined, and equally unnerving to have others speaking to them with her left out of the process. Beyond that, the broader implications escaped her. Still, both men waited.

"I need to at least confer with whoever would be negotiating on our behalf," she said. "Beyond that, I need a little more time to think about it." She sipped the water that Angie had brought for Ruby. "Can you be specific about what you will be doing next?" Clarissa looked at Sandy, who struck her as more the planning type than Jack.

"The government is aware of what has happened, at the highest levels," Sandy said, emphasizing the word "highest."

"Executive, Defense, State, all three," Jack added. "Right now, we pursue two paths. We try to use intelligence on the ground to locate them."

"And we wait for them to make the next contact," Sandy said.

"Contact." That word again. It sounded so sterile, more distant than a handshake. What Clarissa wanted was for someone to fly now to Afghanistan, do whatever was needed to find her husband, put a supportive arm around his shoulder, and bring him home. She didn't want to think about opening a process of negotiations or whether Todd would be safe in a rescue attempt.

They kept talking—about where they would route any call from the kidnappers and who would have to be informed—but Clarissa lost her train of thought. Then Jack was reaching toward her, and she backed away before she realized he was handing her something.

"Sorry. I guess I'm jumpy."

He hesitated a moment, then extended his hand again. "No problem. Here's my card," he said. "Call if you need us. And we'll check in with you tomorrow, let you know where we are. Though there may not be any change that quickly."

Clarissa didn't respond to this forecast. She rose to show Jack and

Sandy to the door. Before leaving, Sandy surprised her by giving her a quick hug.

Back in the kitchen, Ruby was already at the stove, preparing a frittata for everyone to share. Ruby, who Todd said had insisted on only fish sticks and apple slices for breakfast, lunch, and dinner for five months when she was eight years old, had become a gifted chef at a Brooklyn restaurant. She prepared dishes Clarissa couldn't pronounce, patient with slow boils and constant stirrings and recipes so complex that Clarissa would have put them through the paper shredder if they'd ever found their way into her kitchen. Ruby went for sauces. *Coquilles St. Jacques. Foie de veau. Canard rôti à la framboise.* Ruby lived with Angie in an apartment crowded with two dogs, garden tools, even a canoe in the living room, and Todd had described her as perpetually disorganized, the kind of person who missed meetings and went out in mismatched shoes. But to her work as a chef, she brought awe-inducing precision.

The doorbell again. Joel Bass, her department's dean, in a suit, shifting his weight from one foot to another. He hugged Clarissa.

"Joel. Did I call you?"

A smile swept briefly across his face like a bird uncertain whether to land—was Clarissa joking? "Remember? You told me you couldn't come in today, and then you told me—what had happened, Todd and all, oh, but Clarissa, this is natural. What a morning you've had. What stress you are under."

"Yes, of course, sorry, come in," Clarissa mumbled, embarrassed, and led Joel into the kitchen. Joel knew Clarissa as so capable, so solid with details. And in fact, she'd always had a shockingly good memory, the kind of memory that sorted and stored facts, faces, and figures while she looked the other way. Now, though, she apparently couldn't recall a phone call she'd made a few hours ago.

They all greeted this newcomer, everyone speaking in hushed, serious voices, even as Ruby offered some coffee and said a frittata was coming. Joel sat next to Clarissa and leaned close. "As long as you want. You know that, of course," he said, and Clarissa had no idea what he was talking about, so couldn't respond.

"A leave of absence. We'll fill out the paperwork later," Joel added after a moment.

The job, Clarissa realized at last; they were talking about her job at Columbia, and the FBI agents had said to keep things as normal as possible, but Clarissa couldn't imagine going to work right now, standing in front of the students, who would surely know—was it even possible to keep secrets these days? And then Clarissa either breaking down and discussing everything, which the FBI would frown upon, or pretending nothing had happened. Which was impossible. "Yes," she said, "that sounds good; that sounds right. Thank you."

Then Ruby was bringing the food to the table, and there seemed to be a lot of it; Clarissa didn't even think she had enough ingredients for all this, so maybe someone had gone out to the bodega while she hadn't been looking? She couldn't stand the thought of eating. In fact, even with the scent of food, she felt an intense, dull pressure growing in the middle of her chest, reaching toward her belly, and she thought she might throw up. Then someone held her by the elbow—it was Bill Snyder; was he *still* here? "Are you okay?" And the kitchen grew quiet as they waited for her reply. Against her will, she'd become a delicate piece of porcelain they all feared breaking.

And at that point, something did break. "Thank you all for coming," she said. "But now I really need, I need to *think*. So kind, but now I need to ask you . . ."

"Are you all right, Clarissa?" Ruby asked. "Do you want to go upstairs and rest? No one would—"

"No, no, I just need, I need some quiet so I can think. Maybe I can—" She took a deep breath. "Ruby," she said. "Would you help me get everyone out?" She realized, as soon as she finished the sentence, that her voice emerged more shrilly than she might have wanted, and that the sentiment sounded rude. But she also knew she had no desire to retract it.

"Yes, yes, of course," Bill Snyder said, and Mikey was also on his feet. Ruby looked dismayed, and a little angry, and frightened; Clarissa could pick out these emotions and wished to ease them, and she saw milder versions of the same emotions imprinted on other faces, especially pity and surprise. But as much as she wanted to help Ruby, help them all, a part of her knew that what she wished even more, desperately needed, in fact, was for everyone to go.

Joel and Bill Snyder left together. Mikey bent to kiss her. "I'll stop by tomorrow." She held his arm for a minute; part of her wanted to cling to Mikey, but clinging to Mikey would be acknowledging how frightened she was by what was happening, and she couldn't acknowledge that, not in a full-sized bite, not yet, so she let go.

"I'll clean up a little, then," Ruby said, but Clarissa shook her head.

"No. Leave everything. Please."

The words were as restrained as Clarissa could make them, but she knew the tone was tough, and Ruby caught it.

"Would you like me to bring you some dinner?" Ruby asked, her face pale.

"Ruby, that's kind of you. I'll be fine, though. I just need a couple hours to gather myself, to think."

Angie seemed most comfortable, and perhaps even relieved, to be kicked out. She squeezed Ruby's arm gently. "You're doing the right thing," she said softly to Clarissa. "You all need time to absorb this."

Clarissa nodded, though she couldn't manage a smile, and she watched as the last of them walked out the door. Then she closed it behind her. Leaning against it, suddenly aware of deep exhaustion, she sank to the floor.

Stela

September 4th

the bells dangling from the top of the front door made a tinny, strident sound. Stela knew she should welcome it since it meant a potential customer, but these days she found it mainly intrusive. Chekhov stirred slightly and glanced toward the door. Stela, less hospitable, looked up more slowly from the paper on which she was writing to see Yvette waving cheerily. "It's K-Love's afternoon of praise. Positive, encouraging K-Love. Send us your blessed stories by phone or—"

"*Please* turn off that Jesus talk, Stela, for God's sake. I can't stay long—dentist appointment. Coffee on?"

"Help yourself," Stela answered as she reached to turn down the radio. No need to bother arguing that the radio station wasn't that bad, and that when hope went on short supply, one had to overturn the dusty furniture and look in every dank corner. She'd just listen later.

Yvette picked up a yellow coffee cup and surreptitiously inspected the inside.

"It's clean, Yvette."

Yvette flushed, then smiled.

"I'm not a crazy, unkempt cat lady yet."

"I know," Yvette said. "I know that."

Chekhov rose languidly, arched her back, hopped off the counter, and disappeared behind the third row of shelves. Yvette poured herself a cup. She set it on a table across from Stela's counter and gingerly pushed Pushkin out of the armchair. "Shoo," she said. Stela slid two books waiting to be shelved—a dictionary of symbols and a children's tale—on top of what she'd been writing. She could tell by the way Yvette's eyes narrowed that in hiding the paper, she'd only served to draw attention to it. Yvette stared as she took a loud sip of the coffee, but she let it sit for the moment. "Anything new for me?" she asked.

"A Mikhail Shemyakin book. Came in yesterday, and in mint condition." Stela pushed to her feet—she'd put on more weight than she wanted lately, and she wasn't even sure how. It seemed only yesterday she was the lithe girl who loved dancing, and then the young mother sprinting after her sons. She moved to the third aisle, finding immediately the volume she wanted, bypassing the new volume on Russian icons, which she knew Yvette wouldn't like.

Yvette took the book eagerly and flipped through the pages. "What a carnival Shemyakin's work is."

"I know you love him. Too ghoulish for me."

"You have to look at the work without the laughter drained from your soul," Yvette scolded. She turned to the inside cover and read aloud, "'To Grandfather Georgi, Merry Christmas with love from Sasha, December 2003.' Oh, Stela. Another estate sale? Georgi who? Do I know the family?"

Stela shook her head. "He lived in St. Louis. His nephew brought it to me."

Yvette looked at Stela skeptically. Then she returned to the book. "I hate the way you get your books; that's what's ghoulish. But this is a beauty. How much?"

"Eight dollars for you."

"Stela. How are you going to stay in business that way?"

"Let me worry about that."

Shaking her head, Yvette rummaged in her purse and pulled out a ten. She rose, placed the bill on the desk and then gestured toward Stela's cell phone.

"Any calls?"

"I'll let you know if there is." Stela found cell phones ridiculous. She kept a cell for one reason only.

Yvette leaned forward and tapped the two stacked books. "So?"

"What?" Stela reached into a lower drawer on the desk and pulled out a green metal box. From inside, she selected two one-dollar bills.

"Who're you writing to now? The president? Another author? The head of Veterans Affairs? Who?"

Stela held out the money to Yvette, who shook her head. Stela sighed and put the dollars on the table. "Every time, we have to argue over the change," she said. "You'd think it was two hundred dollars instead of two."

"Someone I've heard of?" Yvette persisted. "Or someone obscure this time?"

"Not that it's your business."

"Oh, no. Not your son again?"

"Yvette, please."

Yvette raised a hand skyward. "I'm taking that as a no, Stela. And I'm hoping not, because I don't want to see you suffer more."

"Okay," Stela said. "Thanks."

"How much can one mother's heart take? Besides, haven't I known him since he reached here?" She put her hand on her waist. "I know what I'm saying. He's our *haroshi malchik*. He'll come around in time, so you don't need to take years off your life fretting over it."

"Okay," Stela said.

"Water flows, but the rock remains. You are his rock."

"Hmm."

Suddenly Yvette jumped; Bulgakov had rubbed himself against her legs. Stela couldn't help herself; she chuckled. "My sharpest cat," she said.

"Not so sharp if he thinks I want to pet him."

"I think he specifically realizes you don't."

"Wish you'd thin out some of these cats." Yvette settled back into the armchair. "So. If it's not Danil, who is it?"

"Who says it's a letter? I'm practicing my Mandarin."

Yvette laughed. "You could just say you don't want to tell me."

"I don't want to tell you."

Yvette sighed. "But then I'd be forced to remind you that I am not for nothing your closest friend. Here for the easy times and the hard. Always have been. I'm exactly the place to deposit secrets. *If this is going to be a secret.*"

"Okay, okay. I'm writing my memoirs."

"Oh, right, Mrs. Haha. As private as you are?"

The bell clanged again. Stela turned to see Jenni, her long blond hair swinging, her lipstick redder than maraschino cherries, already in midsentence. "Had to run right over and tell you, Stela, dear. Feelin' good, yes, ma'am," she said, drawing out the last word as if she were an auctioneer. "We have a buyer. At least," she chuckled, "I think we do. They don't want to go quite as high as we'd like—the financial climate, you know, the uncertainty in your line of business—but I think it will come in as a not-too-bad offer. I shouldn't be talking out of school since I don't have the details yet." Here she actually giggled, which Stela found unbecoming in any case, but particularly in a middle-aged woman. "But I was in the neighborhood, so I thought I'd stop in and personally give you a whisper. I'll call later, as soon as I get some numbers, and if you like them, well, we'll shout the news from the rooftops. I want you out of this dusty old store, dear Stela. And then maybe you'll let me talk you into selling that old three-bedroom of yours and buying a cute little condo with a view. There are some good deals out there—I know, I know, you don't want to change your addresses in case friends come looking for you, but we can deal with that, Stela, dear. Oh, well, one step at a time. No, can't have coffee," she said, though Stela hadn't offered any, hadn't even spoken yet. "Sorry to be on the run. But you have to work twice as hard to make half as much money these days." She kissed the air. "Talk to you soon, darling," she said, waving a hand as she turned away.

The door closed behind her and the store seemed for a moment as if the air had been sucked out of it. Yvette stared at Stela, and then opened her hands to the sky. "The shop? Such a big decision as this, you were keeping from me?"

"There's no decision, Yvette. You see how she is? Not a second to get a word in edgewise."

"You put it on the market and you didn't breathe a word. I told you even before I told my ex-husband when I got pregnant."

"Your ex-husband, that *kakáshka*? I'm not sure that qualifies—"

"What will you do if it sells?"

"You think all I can do is own a used bookstore?"

"I think this has been your life for the last twenty years. And there would be trouble if the cobbler started making pies."

"I'm neither cobbler nor cook," Stela said lightly. She rose and idly straightened some books near the door. She didn't really want to go into this. But she turned back to find Yvette staring, demanding with aggressive silence that Stela explain. "Some days this shop is like my prison, Yvette. I imagine the books falling from the high shelves and suffocating me. It's possible, you know. Have you looked around here? Books are living everywhere. I even have them on the back of the toilet in the bathroom now. More than I'll ever be able to sell. So when I die, what'll happen? Someone will come, take them to a recycle center? Labor spent to turn literature into trash: I don't want that to be my legacy."

Yvette shook her head. "Who's talking about dying?"

"It doesn't hurt to think."

"Stela, this is not the moment to sell. Danil needs to know where to find you, and the beaten path is the shortest one."

"Thank you, Yvette. I'm done discussing this now."

"Besides, who will I talk to over morning coffee if you move away? What are we, if not family by now?"

Stela, silent, stacked up four books on the counter, arranging them so the smallest one was on top.

"We're just a couple girls from the motherland—we always said that—and we have to stick together." Yvette put down her empty cup and picked up the Shemyakin book, tapping her fingers gently on its cover without speaking for a few minutes before reaching over to squeeze Stela's hand. "You're not healed yet. You're not ready to make a big change. You hear me?"

Stela shrugged.

"Okay. Okay. I'm getting the silent treatment. I have to get going anyway." Yvette stood up. "You'll do what you want in the end. But don't do anything before tomorrow, Stela, promise me that much. We need to talk more, after you've found your tongue again."

Stela ducked her head gruffly in reply.

When the door closed behind her, Stela let out the sigh she'd been holding. She wished she'd been quick enough to figure out a way to cut off the real estate agent before she began spouting information like a busted water pipe. How could Stela discuss this with Yvette before she was sure herself? The shop sometimes felt like a prison hut in Siberia, as she'd told Yvette. But she'd also loved these old books longer and more deeply than she'd loved most people—yes, the stories themselves, but even more, the history of the hands that had smoothed these covers, bent back a corner, underlined a series of words, dripped lingonberry jam on a page. She loved the estate sales that made Yvette recoil. Buying volumes others had tucked beneath their arms and then bringing them back here to their new home made being in her bookstore like a trip to the ocean; it gave her a sense of timelessness. It reminded her that she was nothing more than a comma in a sea of endless sentences. It made her feel less alone. It sucked the salt from her wounds.

She slid the books off the note she was writing. She should have been a writer—she knew how to tell a story, and she loved words. But it was too late for that; all she had now was the letters, so she kept at it, buying stamps in an age of e-mails, using the Internet solely to track down street addresses, sending out letters to everyone she thought of, and never really hoping for a reply. Except from Danil.

And no letters were more futile, probably, than the ones she wrote to her son. But she couldn't stop, no matter what she told Yvette. He was still angry with her, she suspected. He might not open her letters, if they even reached him via the only address she had. And yet, he was her son; of course she wrote. She kept no copies of her letters, but she suspected if she could look at them as a whole, they would parallel the path of her grief.

It was crazy: the dead son she could visit. She could rant and cry over his body below the ground and try to come to terms with the loss. The other one, alive, had slipped entirely from her reach. Sometimes even, immediately upon awakening, she confused in her mind who was gone and who remained; she imagined calling the youngest to lament over the passing of the oldest.

"Yvette just came in," she wrote now to Danil. "She asked about you as always. She is moving more slowly but has the loyalty of a collie, though please don't mention that comparison to her. If you—" She crossed out the last two words and rewrote: "When you come home, I'll make you pirozhki and invite her to dinner."

She put down her pen and went to pour herself another cup of coffee, placing a sugar cube on her tongue; she still found it comforting to drink coffee in the old way. "We are having an Indian summer, which Yvette calls a St. Martin's summer, and she's explained why, but I've forgotten. I am grateful for this last breath of—" She crossed out the last line. Why should she discuss the weather and dance around the real topic? This was her son; he'd come from within her own body.

"Oh, Dani," she wrote, "we are left behind, you and I. There is no one else with whom I can recall that decade and a half of years rich with your childhoods, that time for which I feel such nostalgia. No one left but you who I can love in such an unprotected way. I miss you."

She paused, chewing on the end of her pen, and began again. "I wish you could have seen the face of the staff sergeant who gave me the details. I cannot believe he lied to me. Besides, Dani, if I accept this as a lie, how much else would I have to question?" She stopped, reread the last three sentences, and, hating them, wadded up the paper. She would start over. Which was fine. Famous authors spent years perfecting their books, after all. She could spend a few more weeks on a letter to her last remaining son.

Grief had changed her. The old Stela had vanished, erased by a war "over there," though in a different way than her sons. First she'd been angry, and that anger had driven Dani away. But she'd understood at last that if she was to get on with what was left, she had to stop clinging to the past. And that was what she needed to tell her son, that alone, if she could find a way to slip the other differences between the pages of a forgotten book.

She remembered how frightening it was to be young and be forced to imagine the inner lives of one's parents. There they were, crazy or disappointed or bitter, sagging in spirit as well as in body. Who wouldn't run from that? She empathized with Dani; she could understand why he fled.

But whom else did she have to explain things to? Sitting there, surrounded by words, searching for the right ones, she took a clean sheet and tried again.

Danil

anil heard the doorbell ring, but he chose not to acknowledge it. He couldn't have been sleeping more than a couple of hours; he needed more. He willed his eyes to stay closed even as he heard a key in the door, and then Joni's voice.

"Morning, Dani. Or actually, afternoon."

He groaned and rolled over.

"Time to get up," Joni said.

"Give me a pass, Joni," he said. "I worked late."

"I'm not sure it's work unless you get a paycheck," Joni said lightly.

"Remind me again why I gave you a key?"

Joni laughed and sat on the only comfortable chair in Danil's apartment. "A cup of coffee," she said, extending her arm, then setting the cup on the rickety table when he didn't acknowledge it. "You're welcome. And here are the latest three letters from your mom." She shook her head. "These letters . . . but that's another topic, Dani. Today I come bearing news, and I don't have much time. I'm on lunch break."

Dani and Joni had met in school seven years ago, before he'd dropped out. She had become a web designer, with an eye for color, a wide streak of practicality, and a brain for business. He was both pleased and amazed that they'd stayed friends, even as he'd grown more solitary, more isolated. "Send me an e-mail," he said.

"Hand that line to someone who thinks you read e-mail."

Dani kicked off the covers and moved his legs to the floor, planting his feet, propping up his head on one arm.

"Your friend Eli stopped over," Joni said.

Danil sighed. "He's not exactly a friend."

"Remind me again why he has *my* address? And why he doesn't know where you live now?"

Danil sat up. "You didn't tell him, did you?"

"If I had, he'd be here already. Listen, he said to give you this. Apparently your work has shown up on some blog site, and some gallery owner is trying to find you. Eli says the guy wants to give you a show."

"How did Eli get this?"

"Trolling blogs? Maybe the guy wandered into his tattoo gallery. How do I know? Anyway, here's his e-mail address and cell-phone number. Contact him."

"Yeah. Whatever. I mean, thanks, Joni. I appreciate you bringing this by."

"But?"

Danil reached for the coffee cup and swallowed a gulp. How many people in your life understood you with only a gesture, an expression, maybe a half-dozen words? The reasons he couldn't do a gallery show were too complex to explain to her, and to try would involve breaking a promise. "I'm just not sure I want to be in a gallery, with all its

expectations and requirements, with people who don't know anything about me or my brother—and don't really want to know—
judging me based on shit that doesn't mean shit," he said.

"Shit that doesn't mean shit?" She leaned closer to him. "*That's*
bullshit, Dani. You get your stuff in a gallery, with more eyes on it.
Ultimately, the rest doesn't matter."

Almost always, Danil thought, Joni saw through him.

"That window?" She rose, pulled back the drape. "Every time I've
ever been here, it's been curtained. And the refrigerator?" In two
steps, she reached and opened it. "Damn close to empty. Dani. You're
not doing too good. Why would you pass this up?"

"I have a job, you know," Danil said. "I paint office and living
spaces."

"Are you kidding me? When's the last time you did that? Besides, that's not the work you want to get old with, is it?"

Danil sighed. He cracked his knuckles one hand at a time.

"I brought you a present." Joni reached into her bag and tossed
him a cell phone. It landed on his lap, but he didn't pick it up.
"Brand new and ready to use," she said. "You can even set up e-mail.
Call the gallery owner. Then open up one of your mom's letters and
fucking reconnect with your family."

Danil shook his head. "Not an option."

Joni shrugged. "Whatever. But while you're on your alternate
trajectory, don't ignore a potential break that I gave up a lunch hour
to help pass on. Opportunities only fall in a person's lap so often."
She leaned over and kissed his cheek, and then waved over her shoulder without waiting for him to respond.

Danil rubbed his palm over his chin and stared at the cell phone. Then he put it and the piece of paper with the gallery owner's contact information on the corner of the only table in his apartment, the table that still held the coffee. "I'll figure it out later," he said, as if talking to the phone itself, and then he headed into his bathroom.

Amin

September 5th

bleach and yeasty bread: the scent of Maiwand Hospital as Amin entered through the main doors. A woman in a burqa squatted by the entrance, holding in her arms a child whose head drooped like a wilted poppy. Amin couldn't be sure if she was begging or simply waiting, but he scrambled his fingers into his pocket and pressed a few Afs into her hand. *"Tashakor,"* she said, barely glancing up.

He'd never been inside Maiwand. Though it was barely adequate, the hospital's primary purpose was to serve as a training ground for Kabul Medical University interns. Amin himself would never come here for care. Of course, he wouldn't go to any hospital in Afghanistan for anything serious—better to India, or the States if possible. Even Pakistan. Backward, violent, filled with war-battered souls: what was it about this country that drew him beyond all logic? He'd been educated abroad and could have stayed. Yet he found himself rooted to this soil. Whatever he hoped to accomplish lay here, along with whatever debt he owed.

To his right, in an office with huge windows, Zarlasht sat at a large desk. One other woman sat at a second desk across from hers.

Amin strode into the office. For a moment, she didn't glance up, focused on her paperwork. Then she saw him, and her surprise registered. "*As-salaam alaikum*," she said, her expression turning formal.

He stood without speaking. Zarlasht glanced toward her colleague, who nodded and left the room. She then looked toward Amin, silent. Though he distrusted her, her self-confidence struck him as impressive.

"An American woman was supposed to meet with Mr. Barbery the day he was taken," Amin said. He took a paper from his chest pocket. "A nurse. He was going to help her, but he cannot. Here is her name. She wants to visit hospitals. I'd like you to arrange a visit to Maiwand."

She laughed. "An American woman nurse? In this hospital? Do you think that's appropriate?"

"She will dress appropriately. She wants to help improve our medical practices. But that part doesn't matter to you. I'm acting on behalf of Mr. Barbery. I'd like you to arrange it for an afternoon sometime in the next week."

Zarlasht narrowed her eyes, studying his face for a moment. Then she looked down at the paper silently. Finally she nodded. "Thursday would probably be fine. In the women's and children's wards only, of course."

"Good," he said, but he didn't move.

"There is something else?" she asked after a moment, a note of challenge in her voice.

"The motivation," he said. "It's a little confusing to me. Was it accidental or half intentional, a target of opportunity? Or was this your sole intent from the start?"

"What are you talking about?"

"Todd Barbery is a good man," he said.

"Yes, I know."

"No. No, you don't. He loves this country, Allah save him. At least up until this week, he did. And he's been foolish at times. He's failed to discern. But he is a good man."

"I heard what happened. I am sorry. I meant to come by and say—"

"But whether or not he is good," Amin interrupted, "that is not relevant to you. What is relevant, what you should know, is that aid workers are not soldiers."

"Of course I know."

"They are not politicians, and they are not ousted leaders."

"I realize—"

"And if all the aid workers are driven out of Afghanistan—"

"But why are you telling me—"

"Todd Barbery," Amin spoke over her, "would never abandon this country, no matter what. But his big boss, his emir back in America, and the other emirs, they will finally say no. Do you understand that? And if all the aid workers are driven out, this will not be a good thing. Not for this hospital—how much foreign money have you received here? Not for the women. Not even, ultimately, for you."

"Of course I know this," she said, rising from her seat as she spoke. "You think this is something I can control? Have you forgotten the country from which you come? Have you forgotten how little we women mean here? How quickly they muffle our voices, if they let us speak at all?"

"You have ears, at the very least."

"Which do me no good now."

"And you also face threats," Amin went on as if she hadn't spoken, "because this country is not ready to smile and bow to a progressive woman, is it? In Afghanistan, progressive women must also be wise, playing one side against another so they can stay safe. Passing on information if needed. That could be motivation, I guess."

She glared at him. "Your implications insult me."

"Really? I was trying hard to be polite."

"I have no connection to criminal elements."

"In our country, politics and crime are wedded."

"Who took him? And why? Those are the questions you should be trying to answer if you hope to win his release."

"Those are the questions I'm trying to answer, Zarlasht."

Zarlasht gestured to the door. "I request that you leave."

Amin studied her face silently, trying to assess whether he could extract any information at all from her, or if he was, for the moment, forced to count a delivered warning as enough.

A young female medical student opened the door. "Zarlasht *jan*, an ambulance has just arrived. A boy stepped on a mine and—" Her words were drowned out by a mother's wailing. The nurse left the office, leaving the door ajar.

"Stay, then," Zarlasht said coldly. "Sit here alone, if you wish. I must admit the patient."

"Of course. But first." Amin leaned forward so he could speak softly and Zarlasht could hear him above the cries of anguish, which would not abate, he suspected, for some time. "Once before I let someone down."

"I know. We all know." She turned her head and murmured under her breath, "He who has been bitten by a snake now fears a piece of string."

"This time, I won't let a good man be sacrificed to wrongheaded beliefs."

"It is not my business," Zarlasht said, "but you know you put yourself at risk in this alliance."

"That is my worry. Here is yours: if you had anything to do with it, you had better make sure Mr. Todd is released safely, and soon. If he is not, and if it links back to your family in any way, I will find out. And you will discover you made a mistake."

She narrowed her eyes. "I must go now," she said.

"Of course." He straightened. "I speak out of respect, Zarlasht," he said, allowing his voice to turn conversational again. "I wouldn't bother giving this warning to a man." He inhaled deeply. "Go with Allah," he said as he turned to leave.

Clarissa

September 5th

larissa dimly realized, as she reached for it, that the phone had been ringing for some time. Out of a desire for silence, not conversation, she groggily lifted the receiver. She put it to her ear but did not speak.

"Clari." It was her brother's voice, and he sounded stern. "Clari," he said again.

"Mmmm." She was aware that the scratchiness in her throat betrayed this as her first attempted word of the day.

"Are you okay?"

"What time," she managed, "is it?"

"Almost noon. I'm downstairs. Let me in."

She replaced the receiver and sank back into bed. How nice it would be simply to close her eyes, go back to sleep, and wake up when she wanted to—that shouldn't be too much to ask, should it? But then she heard the bell again, insistent as a crying baby. She swung her legs to the floor. "Patience," she murmured. Still barefoot, she went downstairs and opened the door. Mikey swept her face with his eyes. "I'm fine, only I couldn't fall sleep until about 6 in the morning," she said, adding unnecessarily, "Come in," as he moved past her into the kitchen. "Want some coffee?" she asked his back.

"I'm already making it." He went to the cabinet and poured beans into the grinder on the counter. She watched him a moment, then slipped into the bathroom off the kitchen.

When she emerged a moment later, she saw that Mikey was trying to carry out an unobtrusive inspection. What worried him? That he would find pills or empty wine bottles? She smiled a little at the thought. In fact, the kitchen looked clean; she'd shoved most of the food Ruby had prepared into the refrigerator, leaving the rest stacked on the counter, one container atop another.

"Ruby's gone mad," she said. "She dropped all this off last night. I know she feels helpless and wants to be doing something, but— what am I going to do with all this? Will you take some?"

He glanced sideways at her as he bent over something on the kitchen table; she saw it was the dead insect she'd left there, centered on a paper napkin. She'd forgotten about that. Mikey straightened, raising his eyebrows in a question she ignored.

"How about some of the salads?" she asked. "It's too much, and it really isn't for me. It's food for Todd, even if she doesn't realize that, and I don't want it to spoil."

"What can I do to help?" he asked.

"I'm telling you, Mikey. Take the food. It feels to me like an offering left at a grave."

"Clari," he said, "I know this is hard—"

"Listen," she interrupted. "I really appreciate your coming and all, but I don't want to—I can't do a conversation right now. I haven't even had coffee."

"Let's remedy that." He poured two cups full, brought them to the kitchen table, and sat. "You heard from the FBI again?"

She shook her head. "Not yet. You're my wake-up call."

He gestured with his chin to the center of the table. "What's this?"

"A bug," she said flatly.

"I meant, what's it doing on your table?"

She looked down, took a deep breath, and then raised her eyes to his. His expression—so serious, as though he were waiting for her to explain a concept like God or soul or identity—made her think of when they were children and the evenings when they would slip away from the grown-ups and he would ask her to tell him a story and then tuck his legs beneath him in patient preparation. This triggered an irresponsible and irrepressible desire to laugh, which quickly morphed into a need to cry. The strangled sound that came out instead startled both of them. She took a sip of coffee, waiting to speak until she'd swallowed and taken a breath. "Look at the wings," she said then, sliding the napkin toward him. "Look how delicate they are. They're small as a baby's finger, but veined, and they have this orange tinge."

He didn't glance at the insect. Instead he looked at her, full in the face.

"Oh, God, Mikey. I killed it last night," she confessed. "I didn't intend to. It was buzzing around near my neck, and I sort of reflexively flicked it away, and then it was half dead, so I took a magazine and kind of gently squished the middle, and then . . ." With Mikey, she always talked more than she'd planned. But she didn't want to share everything that the dragonfly had touched off in her.

He sipped his coffee and didn't say anything for a minute. "You know, Todd is still alive," he said.

"Of course."

"This isn't Mom and Dad."

"Jesus, Mikey." She waved her hand, brushing his words away, but also surprised, once again, by how quickly he was able to identify her fears.

"I mean it. You need to trust a little more. They would know if anything . . . We would all know. So he's alive. And he's probably mainly worried about you."

"And Ruby," she said.

"It's always been hard for you to think of the future, Clari. I've watched that immobilize you for a long time. In some ways, I think you were frozen right up until the moment you met Todd. I don't want to see you go back there."

"I am back there," she said, and then she stopped, knowing if she tried to go on, what would come out would be her anger. She was mad at Todd—for putting everything at risk, insisting on continuing his distant, dangerous work, not letting the two of them together be enough, and now for rewriting her own life so drastically.

These weren't the only things she felt, of course. She felt the weight of responsibility, and she felt frightened for him, and heartbroken for what must be his own fear and sense of fragility. The anger was the selfish feeling, the inappropriate one, so naturally it was also the one that forced its way closest to the surface.

Mikey stood watching her. "You have to be careful, Clari, pushing everyone away at moments like this. We're no good isolated, none of us. It's not useful, and we aren't built for it. We have to let light in little by little."

"You're talking about my sending everyone home yesterday?"

"Well, it was awkward, yes." A smile hinted at his lips for a second. "Look, you can treat people any way you want to right now; you've got lots of latitude. But this isn't Lone Ranger time. It's going to go on for a while, and you need support to face it and figure out how to handle it. There's probably going to be a ransom demand. Then what do you do? Do you want to negotiate yourself or leave it in the hands of their so-called professionals? And then this rescue-attempt thing." He paused. "Maybe we should go to Kabul."

She stood. "How do you expect me to figure out how to deal with kidnappers in Afghanistan, Mikey? It's so beyond . . . anything I know. And the stakes are so . . ."

"We need to figure out a regular time to talk with the FBI. We don't know how long this is going to last; we have to have a system in place," he said. "We need to ask more questions. You, Ruby, Todd's boss, and me, too, because you'll need support."

"Okay."

"We need to confer with them every day."

She nodded.

"We're going to feel better once we're being proactive. Not so unmoored."

"Okay. Okay."

"So you'll call? And let me know? Let us all know?"

Suddenly unable to speak, both grateful for and resentful of Mikey's presence, Clarissa stood and, once standing, didn't know what to do with herself. Impulsively, she lifted the napkin and held the insect up to the window.

He joined her. "Looks like a flying red ant to me," he said.

"I'm thinking some kind of tiny dragonfly," she said. "I didn't know we even had dragonflies in Brooklyn."

He heaved an audible breath. "It's a bug, Clari. Throw it out."

She smiled at his vehemence. "Don't worry. I'm not going to give it a funeral," she said.

"So you'll talk to the FBI and give me a call this afternoon?" he asked. She nodded. "All right, then. My work here is done. Now my actual job beckons. And urgently."

"Thanks, Mikey. Really. You've been there for every rough edge I've ever faced."

"And you for me. But . . ." He made a growling sound. "Next time, Clari, open the door? I was ringing that bell for ten minutes."

He leaned toward her and hugged her a little tighter and a little longer than had been their habit in adulthood. Even that gesture, as warm as it was, felt like admonishment, an urging to pay close attention to every one of these critical days.

part two

At least, it is green here,

Although between my body and the

elder trees

A savage hornet strains at the wire

screen.

He can't get in yet.

— JAMES WRIGHT

Reality is a very effective teacher.

— FORMER U.S. DEFENSE

SECRETARY ROBERT GATES

Najibullah

Letter to My Daughters II

September 6th, 1996

O ne final roadblock, one ragtag roadblock more.

The four years, five months, and three weeks that have passed since then have not dulled the memories of that barricade and that night and the near-miss of my efforts, dear daughters, to reach you and your wonderful mother.

The weather was clear, leaving stars visible. It was nearly 2 a.m. I sat in the middle of a three-vehicle convoy. We'd passed safely through four previous checkpoints with the use of a UN-devised code phrase. (My sense of humor still intact, I suggested "Release the Bull," but the sober UN representatives rejected that.) We were down to a few hundred yards and one last scraggly bunch of fighters separating me from my family, and then I would be in the air, long before dawn left its first morning kiss on Kabul soil.

I'd chosen a pinstriped suit for the journey, a serious tie, carefully polished shoes, black socks. I wanted to look like what I felt myself to be: the head of a modern state, still proud, thoroughly disdainful of the quarreling mujahideen who knew nothing about how to rule a nation as complicated as ours, and the fundamentalists who would drag Afghanistan back a century or more.

Most of all, I wanted to look magnificent for my family when I walked in the door of our new home in Delhi. I'd been exiled before; I knew it would not be forever. I believed we would all return, and in under five years. But I wanted to reassure my three daughters, and especially your mother-flower. I knew she felt as sad and angry as I did to leave Afghanistan. I wanted to drop to my knees and apologize to her for my failure to hold on longer; I wanted to comfort her, and to embrace her and you, my daughters. The image of our imminent reunion brought me solace as we drove away from Kabul in the dark.

I had to leave behind much, but I carried in my briefcase a few presents for you. The stuffed bear wearing a hat with a red star that Muski once liked to sleep with; it was among the gifts President Gorbachev had given me for my daughters when we met in the Kremlin. I know you are not a baby anymore, my green-eyed Muski, but you are still my youngest. Also a large jar of dirt scooped from the Kabul ground, smelling of lemon and a lick of Afghan wind. A few photographs of you girls and your mother standing in the Hindu Kush range. I am glad I brought them because I was never able to return to our home, so now, sequestered as I am, I can look each day on your sweet faces. I can look, too, at the mountains of Afghanistan, which I fear I may never see again outside a photograph.

But of course I will see them. My spirits flag a little when I hear the progress the fundamentalists have made in the countryside. Nonetheless, I will not give up. Shoes are tested on the feet, dear daughters; a man is tested in the fight.

On that night, just beyond that final checkpoint, Benon Sevan sat waiting for me on the airfield, his plane having touched down from Pakistan, full of fuel and ready for departure. At first the delay at the roadblock seemed nothing more than a momentary snag, a piece of disorganization. But when I re-

alized that the round-faced devil Dostum was trying to block my safe passage, I became furious. I climbed from the car and yelled. There was a time when I would not have been affronted in this way, but on this night, I could not change their minds. A mere suggestion of a lieutenant cowered before my voice until he found the courage to speak; he insisted that even if he allowed us to pass, we would all be slaughtered at the airport. Begging my forgiveness, he urged me to return to the official residence. Did Dostum truly think I would simply, stupidly acquiesce to such a proposal? The goat, fleeing from the wolf, may spend the night in the butcher's house, but not I, dear daughters. I have grown to manhood in Afghanistan; I have survived. I am not a fool.

When it became clear that the airport was unreachable that night, I insisted that I was the UN's responsibility and must be taken to their compound and protected by them. They, after all, had written my resignation letter and made my exit part of the peace process. They had promised me safe passage to Delhi. As your mother knows, the decision to resign was a hard one; I've always preferred even the swift blow to the swift flight. But I had met their wishes; now they were responsible for me.

They didn't want me, a weight around their necks, but what could they do? After some hesitation, they agreed, and we made the drive back into the capital far sooner than I had anticipated. Arriving at the UN mission, I wanted to contact your dear mother first; I knew she would be worried. But as always, the responsibilities of state demanded attention. I telephoned my generals, insisting they take action to allow Benon off the airplane, and I called Yaqoubi, demanding an explanation for what had happened at the airport. He promised to investigate and get back to me within twenty-four hours.

I remained optimistic, but I could not sleep. As morning dawned, I listened to the music of Ahmad Zahir. Though he failed to find the wisdom to navigate Afghanistan's politics, Zahir was our nightingale, a mixture of Rumi and Elvis. He was of my generation, one year older than I, and so I always felt as if he were mine. I had little time, even as a youth, for matters of play, but I remember attending one of his concerts in Kabul. And I remember the day he died, the schools closing, his songs on the radio: "My grave is lying unknown along the way." However, that night I didn't want to think of another victim of Afghan politics; I played his love songs, like Sultan Qalbah.

The next morning, I gathered myself. I requested a cup of chai, I washed, and I prayed—yes, one can reach Allah without being an Islamist. But by the time I opened the door to my room, the setbacks had already begun. They had murdered Yaqoubi immediately and named it a suicide. Anyone who knew Yaqoubi knew he would never kill himself. He was a brilliant head of the secret police; he beat back my opponents in 1990 when they attempted a coup, and he would have beaten them back again before he took his own life. Then Wakil, my closest aide, crumbled as easily as a khatai cookie, going on television to call me a "hated leader." If he thought this would save him, he was wrong. I spoke to him only once after that. "Though you swoop down on chickens, O kite," I told him, "you have not thereby become a hawk." We never spoke again.

Still, I was hopeful. How long could this go on? Days? Weeks? Perhaps a month or two at the outside. That was my thinking before Rabbani delivered the final blow. Rabbani, the same donkey but with a new saddle, informed the UN that, as interim president, he would not allow me to leave the country, nor would he allow me to leave the UN compound. Not ever. Those were his words. To arrest me would cause an international outcry, but he knew himself to be so weak that he thought to allow me freedom meant his own power would not be secure. A man is only gone when he's under the sod;

since Rabbani couldn't get me there, he locked me up in the UN compound instead. The empty vessel makes much noise; better for both him and us if he'd stayed a harmless theology teacher.

Expediency. Those who betrayed me believed it suited their interests. But they failed to comprehend the future. This has always been one of my gifts, dear daughters. I have a long-range view. I even called Bush after the Wall fell to warn him that now that the Reds were finished, the problems would be with the Greens. By this, I explained, I meant those who fight under the green flag of the Islamists. I offered my partnership; together we could suppress the fundamentalists before they became too strong. I could strive for greater national unity, not divisions based on ethnicity or extremism. I thought a world leader such as he would understand, but Bush failed to act.

So here I sit. What is the pattern of my days? Too unchanging for my curious mind. Sometimes I feel like a caged lion with little to do except eat, sleep, welcome visitors, and try, as always, to behave in a way that would make you proud. At least they supply me with treats and keep my cage gilded. My sleeping quarters are simple, but my bed is softer than many I've known. I have a room for greeting visitors, a couch, a few chairs, a television set, and a radio. The two UN policemen who "guard" me are pleasant enough. Young Amin takes care of my meager needs, bringing me tea and food, showing in my guests. At first I feared he was sent by one of those camel-dung spiders to kill me or at least spy on me, but no, he seems to truly believe I should still be president. "You are a large leader pinned in a small region," he tells me. By this time, I speak to him as though he were a son.

Sometimes I have foreign visitors, and sometimes they dare to ask me if I regret, if my conscience bothers me regarding acts against my enemies. Regret! It is hard for me to take them seriously when they ask this. These naive children do not understand that this is a clash of values. How long will it take them to learn the fundamentalists will destroy their way of life if unstopped? Have these outsiders or the Afghans themselves forgotten so soon the benefits I brought? Freedom of speech, the multiparty system, an independent judiciary. I've allowed for political differences of opinion and given women full rights. Yes, I had to strong-arm the past at times to prepare it to meet the future. But it was a healthy future I aimed to create.

I say to those who would condemn me: look not only at what I accomplished, which should be enough. Look at who I am. I studied for ten years to be a doctor, interrupted by a prison sentence for my political convictions. Ten years. Why would I spend one-fifth of my life on these studies? Because I dreamed of bringing health to our country. Only when I realized I could achieve more toward that goal as a leader did I abandon my plans to be a medical doctor. And I retain those goals still. How I laughed, dear Heelo, when you urged me to publicly announce I was forsaking politics to set up a medical clinic abroad. You hoped that would mean I could finally leave Afghanistan and join you all in Delhi. Do you remember what I said? First I joked that I could not leave just as I was regaining popularity among my countrymen. Then I told you that, to a football player in the middle of a game, his fans' support is very important. "I am still in the game," I said. "Do not give up on your player." And you haven't, none of you.

When I am not with visitors, my project now is to translate The Great Game *into Pashto, and I am adding a chapter from my times to update the book, since it ends with the fall of tsarist Russia in 1917. I also work out almost daily in my small gym. I will send you my exact body measurements in my next letter—I will be strong and fit when I'm reunited with you all. I hope you are keeping yourselves in shape and will be the same! I only wish I could swim in Lake Qargha as I once did, battling the swells, then stopping to drink* chai *and eat goat roasted over small gas cookers. Those fond days.*

But then I remind myself this is better than when we had to run up and down the stairs for our exercise, so sharp were security concerns. I've achieved much; Allah willing, I will achieve more. But I will not speak further in my own self-defense. Others will do so in time, I am sure. Our people, and the world, will understand eventually what repression and civil war really mean. Allah forgive and save them.

I miss you, my girls, and your precious mother. I can sometimes almost taste the sweet cakes that dear Heelo would bake for me; your cakes, Heelo jan, were becoming better and better, and I can only imagine that you are by now a master. Onie, I miss our Ping-Pong matches, and dear Muski, I miss when we would sing together "Sta de stergo bala wakhlom." I miss our geography lessons, the dinner-table discussions about your dreams and goals, and everything about my dear Fati, your mother.

But we will endure. Inshallah, I will soon be with you; this poor government that has refused me exile doesn't have long to last. So we will see each other again, maybe even within weeks, and then I shall challenge you to a game of carrom and I will share the Hindi movies that have become my favorites while here and we will eat gulab jamun and laugh until the tears come.

Only a little bit longer, my three girls. But every day until then, I am sending love to you and, as always, to your astounding and wonderful mother,

Najib

Todd

September 7th

Waking.

Exhale.

Waking.

Long inhale.

Waking, translucent dreams trailing behind like crumbs left over from a feast.

Awake.

Awake now in the dark. And knowing right away where he lay: on a mat on the floor in a two-bedroom house with the spit of a front yard in an unfamiliar province. Not alone. Two other men slept in the next room, and a third stood outside, the overnight sentinel. Three men among those who had kidnapped him.

And then thinking how wonderful it would be to wake and feel disoriented and not immediately know. To wonder for at least a moment if he was stretched next to Clarissa, or at the guesthouse in Islamabad, or running late for a meeting in Kabul, instead of wondering only if this would be his life's last bed. To forget for a few more heartbeats. To let the oblivion of sleep extend into waking, even briefly.

To his right in the dark, about four feet above the ground, he knew a small window graced the room, maybe fourteen inches square. He glanced that direction but couldn't make out the opening. The color of tar encircled him, and eyes opened were the same as eyes closed. He wondered on which end of midnight he'd awakened. He was—*had* been—a man of Skype and Internet, of multiple time zones and hotel wake-up calls, room service for breakfast: coffee, a toasted English muffin, and one egg scrambled, please. Now he was caught within a village with neither streetlights nor headlights, adjusting to a rhythm of life that lacked connection to the world beyond. Frozen in far simpler, crueler times.

As soon as he'd seen that window, he'd imagined crawling out, and he'd forced himself not to stare so the guards wouldn't follow his gaze and decipher his thoughts. But it would be difficult to avoid awakening the men in the next room, and what of the one in the courtyard? The compound was encircled by a tall wall topped with barbed wire. And even if Todd somehow, magically, got beyond that, where would he go? He knew the landmarks of Kabul, but here? Upon arriving, during the brief trip between the car and the residence, he'd seen that this compound was separated from all others by a field of green that stretched at least a mile; he didn't know what was grown there or, more importantly, who lived in those other houses, what kind of people. He didn't even know the name of the village. He'd asked, but the question had floated in the air until it finally sank to the ground, unheeded.

Through the thin walls, Todd heard a guard in the next room give a quiet snore. He put the fingers of his left hand to the socket of his closed left eye and then ran the tips up to his eyebrow, around to the outer edge of his eye, and down to his cheekbone. His body felt warm under the scratchy wool blanket, but his cheeks were cold from the air. He turned his hips to the right and then to the left as if trying to free them. This body in captivity was all he had left now; he needed to keep it healthy and limber and strong if he could. They'd taken his watch, his wallet, even his Western clothes. Each morning since the kidnapping, he'd awakened feeling disconnected from himself, and not only in a physical sense. Out of touch with his own identity. He'd become unimaginable to himself. The captive, the victim. The infidel.

Todd had always been proud of being logical, even if logic was, as someone once said, the art of going wrong with confidence. But now his ability to reason functioned oddly. In the hours and days since the kidnapping, his mind seemed to be working overtime, running up and down as if through the labyrinth of Tora Bora caves. Yet his thoughts were rebellious and disjointed, refusing to flow together easily.

He'd thought of Clarissa and Ruby and what their days must be like now, and how hard this must be for them. He thought of that often. He'd remembered a recent conversation with Clari. "Youth and entertainment. Those are the kings in our culture," he'd said. "So there's built-in obsolescence, simply in the act of aging. That's not true over there. You can be over forty and still be accomplishing something with your life." He cringed, thinking of it. How ridiculous had he sounded? How much more obsolete could he be than now, kidnapped, powerless and helpless?

He'd thought, in an endless loop, what an idiot he'd been to have gotten nabbed in the first place. He should have been paying closer attention. There had to have been signs—there were always signs. No kids at the ice-cream stand, the look in the eyes of the man in front of him: Had it been significant? How often had he counseled newcomers to stay alert? "Attention is your best form of protection," he'd said. "Don't become complacent." And yet he'd allowed himself to be preoccupied.

He'd thought of Amin, who had to feel worried but also, on some level, pissed off with this American who refused to listen and insisted on solo ice-cream runs. He wished he could have Amin's advice now. His own thoughts were scrambled. He concentrated, trying to envision Amin.

Should I risk it? Should I try to escape?

Not now. You don't want to get caught and anger these men, or end up in worse hands. Just stay alert.

Only one of his captors spoke more than a dozen words of English, and that one, who called himself Sher Agha, appeared infrequently. He'd told Todd negotiations for his release were under way. He'd told Todd the negotiations were going badly. Todd had asked if he could send a message to his family. Sher Agha had said he'd consider it.

Todd removed his arms from under the blanket, stretched them into the dark around him, reaching high, and then made a couple halfhearted punches into the air. He swung his arms in circles, feeling the movement all the way to his shoulders. After a few minutes, he slipped them back under the blanket. He crossed them over his chest and imagined holding Clari. But he didn't want to think too much about what he missed. He wouldn't have been home yet, anyway. Maybe he'd get lucky, and a deal would be reached so he would be home in a couple weeks, as he'd originally planned.

He felt a momentary lifting of his spirits—was that possible? There'd been a number of previous kidnappings in Afghanistan, so there existed a pattern, he suspected, and he wished he knew it. He imagined a manual, a numbered to-do list for kidnap victims, highlighted and with exclamation points for emphasis. Keep up your spirits. Wait with grace. Continue eating! Don't imagine the worst!

He suspected prayer would be advised, but he didn't know how to pray in a way that meant anything to him. He did know, however, how to feel grateful. If he listed the reasons for gratitude, as a Muslim recited the ninety-nine names of Allah, it might suffice.

Inhale. Grateful he wasn't hurt, or in pain.

Inhale. Grateful that his fear had been paralyzing only at the beginning—the explosion, the smoke, men with hidden faces grabbing his shoulders, shoving him into a waiting car, the sense of forced birth into something unwanted.

Inhale. Grateful the worst kidnapper had vanished to somewhere else, the tall one who spit at his feet and hissed a few mangled sentences, the words *"Amrikaee"* and *"kafir"* breaking free.

Inhale. Grateful that the rest of them—so young they would be college students in his country—seemed to regard him primarily with curiosity instead of rage. This led him to feel more empathy for zoo animals than he ever had before, and he was once tempted to scratch his privates and stuff food in his mouth with one hand as the guards sat furtively watching him. But even that thought served a purpose, bringing him brief amusement. They didn't know what to make of him, these young Islamists. They seemed more fearful of him than he was of them. As if he might contaminate them.

Contaminate. Something he was not so grateful for: the food. They shared the same food they were eating, but it had left his stomach in tatters, necessitating urgent runs to the outhouse, the use of quick, elaborate hand gestures and then a dash across the courtyard, hoping they wouldn't misunderstand, wouldn't misconstrue this as a ham-handed escape attempt and shoot him.

But okay, grateful again. Inhale. Grateful that they didn't misunderstand; that they didn't shoot him.

Inhale. Grateful the weather was not too cold.

Inhale. Grateful his kidnappers regarded him as precious cargo that they didn't want other kidnappers to pirate. One of them called him "the Honored Guest"—though in a tone that held sarcasm—and in fact they hid him like treasure as they traveled from one safe house to another. Though he wished he could look out the window instead of being rolled into a carpet or shoved on the floor beneath a blanket, it was a price he could pay.

Inhale. Grateful that, though they sometimes poked his ribs with the end of their guns instead of using words to tell him to move, or stand, or stay still, they hadn't, after those first few hours, held a weapon to his head. Exhale.

Inhale. Grateful no one had forced him to make a videotape.

Inhale. Grateful that he was in good health when taken.

Inhale. And that his vision was fine. He'd heard about hostages robbed of needed glasses who suffered as both their inner and outer worlds blurred.

He didn't have a plan yet, and he wasn't grateful for that, but he hoped one would come to him eventually. And then there would be cause for more gratitude.

He tried to let thankfulness flow through him, even as his stomach argued against it. He tried to focus on the sound of his breath, proof that he still existed, and to rest while he could. But just as he reached the edge of blessed sleep—the ultimate gratitude right now—the call to prayer resonated through the room from a nearby mosque, followed within minutes by the stirring of his kidnappers pulling themselves sluggishly to their feet, rising into a fresh day, another day of his captivity, to pray.

Clarissa

September 7th

S he arrived early. She wore sunglasses, the classic incognito look, and walked directly to the side of the office, out of sight of the windows. In the days before Todd, and even afterward, with him gone so much, she'd become surprisingly connected to the staff at Green-Wood—even more than to her colleagues at Columbia, in some ways. Glasses of wine, evening events, all that. But this crisis had left her lurking at the edges of her own life, hiding from the people she normally embraced. She stood waiting, trying to let herself be soothed by the high wind in the trees and the chatter of the monk parakeets that nested in the Gothic Revival front gates.

She only had a moment before Penny came out of the office. "Can you believe this weather? Wonderful day for grave rubbings, isn't it?"

Clarissa's stomach spasmed as she summoned a smile. They had no idea what was happening, not Penny nor anyone else here, which was fine in the sense that it hadn't—not yet, at least—impacted her occasional work at Green-Wood. Still, it felt like lying.

She put in ten hours a month for a minimal salary making tracings of the gravestones and writing reports on how they should be preserved. Grants were applied for, and sometimes the restorations were made. She loved the work, a nice companion job to teaching, research, and writing. It seemed to her natural to love both the urban environments that daily rubbed history away and the fragments within the city that held some permanence, hints of old stories. She'd been working at Green-Wood so long, and so successfully, that they pretty much let her set her own hours. No one felt surprised to see her show up at any moment. Normally, she set aside time for a cup of coffee with whoever was in the office. But she couldn't bear small talk these days. She couldn't bear to hear someone ask "What's new?" and to try to offer some banal answer.

"No work today," she said. "I'm going for a pleasure walk."

"Even better. This place is so lively in the fall, isn't it?" Penny said. "There's a wedding in the chapel today—the third this month. Once the chic place to be buried, now the chic place to be married. Doesn't that sound like good PR?"

"Put it on Twitter." Clarissa managed a small smile.

"Exactly. Oh, and there's a memorial service not too far from Lola Montez. You might want to head in the Bernstein direction to avoid the crowds."

The roads and walkways of the cemetery all had names like Dawn Path or Arbor Avenue. But Green-Wood employees and regulars gave each other directions using the grave sites of favorite or better-known "permanent residents."

"Thanks for the tip," Clarissa said. "And here's Ruby," she added, hoping her relief was not too apparent. She gave Ruby a short embrace, introduced her to Penny—"Meet my stepdaughter, Ruby"— and then waved good-bye. Clarissa and Ruby headed up the steps on the other side of the entrance road and along the path that passed

"Our Little Emily." Emily's spot on a rolling lot was marked by a tiny stone and circled by larger headstones, as though she were being watched over by the grown-ups. Made of marble, Emily's small stone, from 1874, was deteriorating badly; though most of the restoration funds were earmarked for well-known residents or Civil War grave sites, Clarissa had developed a fondness for "Our Little Emily" and the family who surrounded her. For a couple of years, she'd been playing with the idea of paying personally to restore Emily's tiny monument.

Ruby wore jeans and a sleeveless shirt. Her hair was pulled back. The weather was fine, but Clarissa, in a light jacket and scarf, had been running cold for days. Once they got away from the office, they had privacy, as she had known they would—even more than in Prospect Park. In the cemetery, passersby avoided one another, walking out of their way to sidestep someone sitting near a grave or strolling along a shadowed path. She and Todd had had their most critical talks in Green-Wood. This was the first time she'd been here with Ruby—in fact, she realized, the first time she and Ruby had gone anywhere alone together. Clarissa wondered why she hadn't suggested something before, a play or lunch.

"Sorry I didn't want to talk at the house," Clarissa said. "The house has begun to feel . . . hard. You know?"

Ruby nodded without conviction, her lips a compressed and colorless line above her chin. She leaned toward Clarissa in a confiding way. "Clarissa?"

Clarissa took Ruby's arm. "Yes?"

"I hope you don't mind me mentioning something."

"You can say anything."

"We never talked about this before, but . . ." Ruby looked out at the horizon for a beat, "well, you know, I don't think of you as my *mother*, of course. And not even really my stepmother. I mean, I was already fully an adult by the time you met my dad, so I think of you as my dad's wife. And he's happy, and I think it's great, really. It's just that it doesn't have much to do with me, if you know what I mean."

"Oh," Clarissa said. "Well. Of course."

"Our age difference, what is it? A dozen years? It just feels jarring to me when you introduce me that way."

"But of course that's not—" Clarissa broke off, releasing Ruby's arm. This hadn't been what she'd been expecting Ruby to say. But at least it was honest, she told herself, knowing that she was looking for the silver lining.

"I'm sorry," Ruby said. "Everything is just so intense. . . ."

"I understand. I'm glad you told me," Clarissa said, recovering her composure. "Frankly, 'stepdaughter' never felt quite right to me, either. But 'Todd's daughter' seems wrong, too."

"Then just Ruby is fine."

They walked in silence for a moment. "You feel like walking, or sitting?" Clarissa asked.

"Sitting, I guess," Ruby said. "I've never taken a meeting in a cemetery."

Clarissa smiled. "Let's go over here." She led the way to the John Anderson family mausoleum, 1864. The steps were a pleasant resting place on nice days. The East River stretched in front of them; New Jersey could be glimpsed to the right through the trees. She inhaled the air and pulled a thermos and two Styrofoam cups out of her bag. "Warm tea," she said, pouring for both of them.

Ruby took hers without meeting Clarissa's eyes.

"I like cemeteries. It's probably weird. But I spent some quality time in them when I was younger."

Ruby nodded. "Your parents. The car accident."

"Yeah. I kind of fell apart, and it lasted for a few years. I used to go talk to them whenever things got rough. Sometimes I'd leave them notes. Anyway." She took a sip of tea. "How's Angie?"

"Fine."

"You're still going to work?"

Ruby nodded.

"Good. Are you sleeping okay?"

"Clarissa," Ruby said, "I think I should go see my grandmother and tell her what's happening."

Todd's mother lived in a home for the elderly and recently had been diagnosed with Alzheimer's. She spent hours playing cat's cradle with a string, her fingers' flawless muscle memory of a childhood pastime surviving the loss of short-term recall. Watching her fingers move beneath her calm face, Clarissa found her beautiful. Even with the fading of her mind, she seemed to remember who Clarissa was, at least in general terms, although sometimes she called her Mariana, the name of Todd's first wife.

"I telephoned the home yesterday," Clarissa said. "I wanted to check in on her."

Ruby looked surprised, then caught herself. "I think Grandma would want to know what's going on," she said.

"I talked to Maggie, her primary caretaker," Clarissa said. "I told her about Todd; I felt I had to be honest with her. Maggie believes we have to weigh telling your grandmother against the anguish it's going to cause, even if she forgets a few hours later."

"I don't know about that," Ruby said firmly.

"Everything is so uncertain," Clarissa said, "Maggie thinks we should wait. I think it's what Todd would want, too."

"Well." Ruby took a sip of tea as if to gather herself. "Let me think about that," she said.

"Okay."

"And then, something else," Ruby said then. "If there's a chance to get him out, we need to do it."

"Of course."

"There are three ways, as far as I can tell. He escapes, he's released, or he's rescued. So I need to understand your reasoning on refusing the rescue."

Clarissa took a sip of tea, hoping to slow down, defuse, the conversation. "The permission they want is so open-ended, Ruby. Soldiers with guns going in somewhere in the middle of the night would put Todd's life in danger, and maybe unnecessarily."

"Most of the time, aren't they pretty accurate?"

"Bill says innocents are killed all the time—usually Afghans. I don't want to risk it, not while we still have a chance for negotiations to succeed."

"Negotiations with whom? We aren't sure even who's got him or how sincere they are about wanting to talk. What bargaining chips do we have in our pockets anyway? We have no serious money to offer."

"Ruby, your father has always trusted Amin, and Amin says he thinks he can pull this off, get Todd out. He says we should wait."

"So let Amin talk. But we have to let them rescue Dad if they think they can."

Clarissa reached to touch Ruby's fingers, which were wrapped around her cup. She felt Ruby tighten, so she withdrew. "I keep asking myself, what would Todd want? I believe he would want this resolved without the military involved."

"What Dad would want," Ruby was almost yelling, "is to be safe. To be home."

"Of course. But what's going to get him home? What's going to keep him safer? Negotiations or guns?"

"That's a major oversimplification." Ruby put her cup down on the cement step.

"Ruby. Your viewpoint is critical here. Whatever we call each other, we're the family. Together. You and I."

"Okay. Well, okay." Ruby took a deep breath. "I'm glad to hear you say that. So: I want to allow them to attempt a rescue whenever they feel they should. I want to give them that trust."

Clarissa looked to the left, away from the water, further into the cemetery. Someone had attached yellow and orange helium-filled balloons to a bush near several tombstones, and they bobbed cheerfully in the breeze. "I'm afraid of the kind of action they're talking about, Ruby. Can you understand that?"

"That's just baseless, Clarissa. What do *we* know?" Ruby moved her arms in a circular gesture. "Look at us. We're sitting in a Brooklyn cemetery, theorizing."

"I think Todd would want me to trust his colleagues. Both Amin, and Bill Snyder, who also trusts Amin."

"What about the people who are trained to look out for Americans in Afghanistan?"

"Looking out for American interests isn't the same thing as looking out for Todd."

Ruby was quiet for a moment. "Angie thinks we should give them the okay," she said.

Clarissa stood. "You can see the water from here. Look."

Ruby watched Clarissa but did not stand to look at the view. "You said my voice was equal to yours."

"It is."

"But you aren't actually listening."

"I *am* listening. I just want to give Amin a few more days. Can you go with that?"

"Jack says everyone agrees to this. It's pro forma. The government doesn't even ask when the kidnap victims are soldiers, but they have to if civilians are involved. Even so, everyone says okay."

"When did he say all that?"

"He called me."

"Doesn't it seem to you that he's spending an inordinate amount of energy trying to get an okay for a possible rescue attempt?"

"Clarissa, he must know something that makes it important."

"Then he needs to tell us."

"But it's probably not definite, so he feels he can't. 'Purposely murky.' That's the phrase he used with me."

"Well, I need a little more transparency. That's the phrase I'd use with him."

"And that's it?"

Clarissa sighed. "For now. For now, that's it."

Ruby stood up. "I've got to get to work."

"I was hoping we could . . . we could walk a little. Talk a little about something else."

"There is nothing else right now, Clarissa. And I'm running late."

Ruby left without looking back. Though they weren't far from the entrance, it was easy to get lost in Green-Wood. Even Clarissa sometimes still did. "Stick to the right," Clarissa called after her.

Clarissa rose and headed deeper into the cemetery. Ruby seemed so certain—more certain, actually, than Clarissa—about the way forward. So why was Clarissa holding her ground so stubbornly? And what if her gut feeling was wrong? What if Todd was killed while American troops were waiting for an okay from some clueless wife back in Brooklyn?

. . . humans are delicate so keep it safe humans are impermanent so take the risks humans are transient so soak in the details . . .

She had wandered into a part of the cemetery she didn't know well. She ran her fingers along the rough top of an old tombstone and then knelt before it to read the lines engraved. They were still barely legible. "But as for me, for you, the irresistible sea is to separate us, As for an hour, carrying us diverse—yet cannot carry us diverse forever." She recognized the lines. Walt Whitman, claimed by Brooklyn, still memorized in its classrooms. "Yet cannot carry us diverse forever." She repeated the lines aloud. And marveled, again, at the perverse power of a cemetery to bring her comfort.

Danil

September 7th

One foot jammed into the opening between the bars of the rusting gate, Danil shoved aside a vine to tighten his grip. He hoisted himself, hovered in midair for a tremulous inhale, and pushed over, managing to clear the barbed wire as well as the pointed ends of the iron posts. An angel flight, he called it, both risky and exhilarating. He was not as agile as he'd been in his twenties, and he'd torn his shirt more than once doing this exact maneuver.

Landing on the ivy-coated ground, he moved quickly away from the street. If he were spotted in the wrecked grace of Admiral's Row, once the jewel of Brooklyn Navy Yard housing, he could face a trespassing charge and a fine he couldn't afford to pay. Yet there was something so symbolically right about what he did here that he continued to chance it. He wasn't the only one: urban explorers, photographers, and the occasional graffiti writer made their way in, too. He'd never seen anyone but sometimes spotted what they left behind: a discarded water bottle or film box, a tag.

Heading for the third house in the row, he climbed up decomposing steps covered with dried leaves and bark. He passed through the vine-claimed front door and headed cautiously up to the second floor. Admiral's Row, once an oasis of stately entryways and arched windows for high-ranking military officers, was built in the late 1800s complete with a skating rink, greenhouse, parade grounds, and a sense of exclusivity. The homes were occupied until the 1970s, but once they were abandoned, the environment immediately began its reclamation work, both destroying and, in Danil's view, enhancing. He'd passed the walled group of crumbling homes several times while biking into the city for work, and it had aroused his curiosity. Finally, about a year and a half ago, he'd decided to check it out. Despite the "No Trespassing" signs, he'd been visiting regularly ever since.

A hole in the roof of the second floor invited a single stream of light into the room. He reached behind a crumbled wallboard and brought out a stack of envelopes. His mother's letters, mostly unopened, about seventy of them. A remarkable collection already. From his back pocket, he extracted the three more Joni had given him and added them to the pile. He'd stopped reading them a long while ago and didn't want them in his apartment, but he felt it would be wrong to throw them away. He hadn't known what to do with them until he'd seen the inside of Admiral's Row. He'd returned a week after his initial visit with the first thick set of letters to deposit.

He also stored here a favorite picture of Piotr, sporting the beginnings of his first mustache. His hair straight and long, he leaned into the camera, his lips parted in what wasn't exactly a smile but a friendly look of acknowledgment. Danil had taken the photo himself, right before Piotr had gone to get his head shaved. "Dumbass," he said aloud to his brother. "For fuck's sake. Why?" He asked the same thing every time he looked at the photo, although sometimes the underlying question varied. He'd refused from the start to visit the lie of his brother's grave, but he'd begun talking to Piotr here.

Danil propped up the photo and leaned back on the heels of his hands, rolling his neck to loosen the muscles. "Sometimes, you know, you shit," he said aloud, "I feel like a war casualty myself. That's why . . ." He shook his head, squeezing his lips together as if to stop the words, stop the thoughts themselves. "Is it wrong if I end up benefiting from it somehow? I mean, maybe Joni's right; I might as well meet the guy. But I also might have to say stuff that will make Mom sadder, or angry, or . . ." He rested his forehead in the palm of his hand a minute. "I really gotta get something together here, bro, or I might as well be buried next to you right now."

He paused, half expecting a sign, something he could interpret as a reply, but nothing came. He laughed then, a little harshly. "Talking to a picture, yeah?" He lifted the photo and tucked it carefully behind the wallboard, next to the pile of letters. "Later," he said, rising.

He hesitated for a moment in front of a ragged opening where a window once had been, looking out into a ruined garden where nothing remained to recall more lively times. Maybe he should open one of his mother's letters, just one. Maybe the most recent. But he hesitated. What could he hope to find there? Certainly not the permission he wanted. He missed his mom, and the way they used to be together. He figured part of her had died with Piotr, just like a version of him had died, too, leaving in its place someone who hung out in deserted buildings looking for signs. "Shit," he said, and he turned and headed down the crumbling stairs.

Clarissa

September 8th

ello. Is this Mr. Todd's wife?"

The voice sounded muted and distant; she wondered if a poor connection could be blamed or if the speaker simply used a hushed tone. "Yes," she said, tightening her grip on the receiver, pressing it more closely to her ear. "It is."

"I am very sorry for what has happened," he said. His English was only slightly accented. And he did, in fact, sound crestfallen.

"Amin?" she said. "Is that you?"

"Yes."

"Oh. I'm so glad to hear from you."

"My people, they are good," he said. "They are generous and welcoming. They will offer a passing stranger dinner and a bed. But Afghans have endured loss and violence and fear. The culture of war has corrupted souls."

"I understand; of course I do," she said. "My husband loved—he loves—your country. And also working with you."

"I was happy to hear Mr. Todd was marrying again, after so many years as a widower. He showed me your picture once," Amin said.

"And I've seen yours." Clarissa remembered Todd telling her that business in Afghanistan, even urgent business, had to be prefaced with a certain amount of complimentary small talk undertaken in an unconcerned tone, as though one had no worries at all. She had to manage, she told herself, to restrain a spill of questions and fears.

"I wish we could have spoken under better conditions."

"We will, one day," she said. "So, Amin. Bill Snyder says you know who to talk to in order to obtain Todd's release."

"I am sorry it has taken me so long."

"So you know who is holding him?" She felt a surge of hope.

"Not specifically, no. But I believe I know where to go now, who to ask. I will try."

As suddenly as it had lightened, her heart sank at his reply. He sounded so tentative. "Yes, thank you. But do you think . . ." She let her question trail off.

"We will be successful," he said after a moment. "*Inshallah*."

Todd had said that word always gave him the comforting sense that the best effort would be made. To Clarissa, if seemed a ready-made excuse: oh, well, God didn't will it. Just at the moment when she needed to concentrate on everything, on the tone and the words and the meaning beneath them, she felt dizzy. "Amin, what do you think about a rescue attempt?" she asked. "I mean, a military rescue. If they can figure out where Todd is."

He made a sound, something like "Oh."

"The Americans want permission from me, and so far I haven't given it," she said. "Is it your sense that we should negotiate first? Or do you think Todd might be in such danger that . . ."

The line was silent for a minute. "Are you there?" she asked at last.

"Mrs. Todd," he said, "I understand how worried you must be. I have a wife, too. I imagine her in this situation. I imagine other wives of good and generous men who have been in your situation. History has shown some of my countrymen to have a cruel streak."

"So you think . . ."

"But Mrs. Todd, it is early." His voice sounded louder now.

"What do you mean?"

"With a rescue attempt, of course people will die. Which people, we cannot be certain. I have not yet tried words like 'honor' and 'justice,' to see if they will work."

"So you think . . . ?"

"I think, *inshallah*," he said, "that we will succeed with the *jirga*. We are a society of relationships, Mrs. Todd; our connections are more powerful than our laws. *Inshallah*, I will bring your husband back."

"Do you think we should offer money? I mean, we don't have a lot, but . . ."

"Let me see what can be done first by talking. Your husband should not have been kidnapped."

"But he's American, and I know—"

"Try not to worry too much, Mrs. Todd," Amin said.

His voice definitely sounded more solid now, though she couldn't believe she was attempting to make decisions based on intonation carried over a long-distance line and from the lips of someone she'd never spoken to before. Gripping the receiver, she paced the room. "My husband told me once that he knew he could count on you," she said, reminding herself as much as telling him. "He said you were the man he would want beside him in a crisis."

"He said that?"

"He did."

The line went silent again. "I will very soon call you or Mr. Bill," Amin said after a moment.

"Yes, please. I hope to hear good news, but I will want to know even if the negotiations begin to look impossible."

"We will believe in success," he said.

"Yes. Todd's daughter and I, we both appreciate . . ." She paused, suddenly overcome with a poorly timed rush of emotion. "We appreciate what you are doing. I know Todd would, too. I do believe in you. I think you can get him home." She paused but heard no response. "Are you still there?" she asked.

Then he spoke; now, again, his voice sounded far away, but she could make out the words. "I will do better than my best, Mrs. Todd," he said, and repeated: "Better than my best."

And that, she told herself as she hung up, was the closest thing to a promise that she could hope for.

Todd

September 40th

awakening in the dark, he found his upper chest knotted like a storm cloud, his cheeks damp as if after rainfall. He touched to feel the moisture, then wept even more in disappointment. Not once so far had he cried, not once. But now his tears had tricked him; since he'd successfully held them at bay, they'd found a way out while he slept. It seemed, in fact, that he'd been crying for a while; the corner of the sheet he hugged also felt moist. And once begun, they showed no sign of abating, though from somewhere he found the self-discipline to weep silently.

Every inhale hurt, too; the tall guard who had vanished, the one full of rage, had returned the day before and had kicked Todd in the right side when he'd been sitting down. Why was beyond Todd's grasp; perhaps he hadn't liked something about how Todd looked, or who Todd was. Another had pulled the hostile guard away, but no one had offered to help Todd. At first he had been nauseated and dizzy; then he'd spit up blood; now he feared broken ribs. The pain felt sharpest about six inches below his underarm. He touched there gingerly and bit his lip to keep from crying out. The guards sleeping in the next room still breathed steadily; Todd hadn't awakened anyone yet, and he didn't want to. While they slept, he was free. Relatively speaking.

Because of that, nights were the best, but they were also the hardest. They were so black here that he felt plunged into nothingness. His sole companion was a ravenous one: guilt. Look what he'd done to his wife and his daughter. He could only imagine what Clarissa and Ruby were feeling; he knew neither one had truly healed from old wounds, Ruby the loss of her mother, Clari of her parents. He knew those wounds had to have reopened now. He hoped Ruby was supporting Clarissa; though younger, Ruby had more brash confidence than his wife. Clarissa hadn't wanted to fall for him; she'd been clear about that. She had to be regretting it now.

He wept for them and for himself: he didn't want to die here. In the middle of the night, he had lost all possibility of magical thinking, all hope for escape or rescue or negotiation; he understood that little by little, the violence against him would increase, and he'd never get out. Seen on the canvas of history, in light of karma, it made sense; it was even fair. How many noncombatants had been injured or died at the hands of American troops? The numbers would never be determined, but they were large enough, he knew, to justify his own death in return, a small down payment on eventual payback.

He cried, too, for Afghanistan. No one would ever believe that, if he could tell them. He loved this country's people, whose faces were etched by want and loss and fear and who still opened their lips to laughter. But he wondered how they could have ceded so much power to young, ignorant men and their leaders, often from outside the country, most of them not simply uneducated but actively disavowing education as if they sensed—and they had to, didn't they?—that knowing more would inevitably disrupt their perfectly constructed, largely false worldviews. It sounded esoteric next to his tears for his family, his freedom, his life, but still he felt it: the loss of this country.

He was fully awake now, and very aware of the pain in his side. After several minutes' focus, he managed to transport himself to Brooklyn, where he saw himself walking down the street with Clarissa, headed for the subway. They stopped at the place on the corner for coffee, and they split an everything bagel. He tried to bring specificity to the way the bagel tasted, the heat of the coffee on his tongue. In his mind, he took Clari's hand and said, "Let's skip work. Let's be teenagers today." In his mind, she laughed and they turned back toward home. Feeling all this almost as if it were truly happening, Todd, lying somewhere in Afghanistan not far from the Pakistan border, smiled.

There was still so much ahead. In some ways, it had all just begun. A new beginning, at his age: How had he failed to appreciate that? This constantly running after something new, it had become a trap. If he somehow could get home, he vowed, he would stay there. He would stop running. He would embellish the contours of his own life instead of trying to color outside the lines. If he had the chance, he would remember something he'd forgotten after the death of his first wife. He would remember how to love what he had.

Stela

September 10th

Dorogoi Mr. Chomsky,

Greetings, or *privyet*, as I would like to be able to salute you; I know you must know your Russian given your parents' background. My name is Stela Sidorova, I am fifty-six years old and immigrated from the Soviet Union with my then husband when I was only twenty years old. We moved to Ohio, where I now own and run a used bookstore. Alone, I might add. My husband, the *chyort*, deserted me nine years after our arrival here. I should have pounded his balls, but he was not a real man, as you are, a man who stayed with his wife and supported his offspring. Oh, well, forgive my frankness as I have forgiven him. At least he contributed to the creation of two little boys, who then became mine alone. And because of him, I learned I must pray to God but keep rowing to shore—an important lesson.

I have many copies of books by you in my shop, more than I will ever be able to sell. But that does not mean you are unpopular with the Russian community here—just the opposite. Most part with your books only when they are dead. Perhaps if you are ever traveling in this area, you will stop in and sign some. It would be a great pleasure to meet you.

But I'd better get to my point, in case you think it is simply for this that I trouble you. I write for two other reasons. One is personal: I am preparing to compose a very important letter to my only surviving son, and so every correspondence is practice for that one. I hope you won't be insulted by my confession. It is only in letters that I feel I can be fully honest, even with myself; perhaps, as a writer, you understand that.

The other reason is about the war. I know you are a member of the intelligentsia and a dissident, two groups which are much smaller in this country than in ours: the country of my birth, the one you must also partly claim. And I know that you are an expert on how governments behave. What do you think: Is it possible that an American military officer would lie to a mother about the death of her son in war? Would the army tell a mother her son was a hero when he wasn't? Would they bury him at Arlington if he didn't deserve to be there?

I hope this question doesn't strike you as naive. I know of course that governments lie; I was born a Soviet, after all. But the soldier who told me what happened to my son seemed so reliable to me, and I'm a good judge of character. I found myself wanting to comfort him, he seemed so sad.

I am not like you, a famous writer and thinker, but I am well read and not an idiot—I have spent years surrounded by these books, so how else could I be? I know you have an excellent brain. I know you are a critic of my adopted government. I know you will tell me there is a possibility I was deceived. But what I am wondering is if you will tell me that it is really likely they would lie to someone as unimportant as me about something so important.

Finally, I must to tell you one thing, dear Mr. Chomsky—or Noam, as I hope I can call you, given our shared heritage and having revealed so much of myself. I say this as a sister from your parents' homeland. If you look like the most recent pictures I have seen of you, you need to trim your hair. It's not that I object to wild hair—my boy Piotr had such hair. But if you are going to criticize the men who sit in boardrooms and government offices, you yourself must look like you've just walked out of one. Put this way, I imagine you see what I mean. So will the barber.

I await your reply. Thank you for your time, and remember the invitation to my store. It is called Bulgakov's Bookshelf. I would be happy to see you anytime, haircut or no.

Iskrenne vash,
Stela Sidorova

Amin

September 11th

min woke into silence. He opened his eyes and let them close again. A moment later came the first syllables of the call to prayer. A sign of the effectiveness of his body clock, which had been set in youth and now virtually never failed to try to raise him at this hour, even when he'd fallen ill or found himself in places where prayer calls would never be heard—although how people could live forever without the dawn call to prayer, without that mystery and meaning, bewildered him.

"Allah is great." The muezzin broke through the darkness, expanding each word into music, carrying the melody of a desert wind on a summer night. Amin rested a hand on his wife's belly, feeling the movement of her breath meld with the praise of Allah. Lingering, he let the sound of the *adhan* soak into his body. He was reluctant often, but today in particular, to fully shed sleep. "Hurry to prayer. Hurry to prayer," came the last admonitions. "Prayer is better than rest." The *fajr* worship time was Allah's favorite, it was said, since one must rise from slumber for it. He rolled from his bed, gave his eyes a moment to adjust, moved to the sink to wash, and then outside to pray.

When he returned inside after finishing, the scent of *chai* greeted him. His wife handed him a cup without speaking; he kissed her forehead. He drank, feeling the tea warm his throat, as she stood silently watching him. It was rare to see her both awake and unmoving. "Mahmoud and the girls are still sleeping?" he asked.

She nodded.

The stiff posture of her back, the rootedness of her feet, made a statement that demanded a response. "I have to," he said.

She shook her head. "No, you don't."

"I have to do everything I can."

"Everything you can from the safety of our home, fine. Traveling into Ghazni, speaking out there on behalf of an American: this is madness. Were you so long away from this country that you forgot?"

"I have to do what I can. He's my boss, and he's human, and he's done nothing wrong. It's not nationality that matters."

"In your mind, yes. But not in theirs."

"What about yours?" he asked. "Would you feel better if it weren't an American I was trying to help?"

She didn't answer.

"It's not as simple as us against them," he said. "It's never been that simple. It's all of us—Mr. Todd, and you, and I, and the others—and among us are some of them. You know that."

She turned and knelt before a wide-mouthed bowl she'd already filled with bread dough. She dove her right hand into the bowl and began kneading. The sight soothed him.

"Us. Them," she said after a minute. "A fine and esoteric argument. It will not help when they ask if you love infidels."

"I can manage their questions." He spoke with greater confidence than he felt. She wasn't fooled.

"Like my uncle did?" His wife's uncle, a policeman in Wardak, had been shot to death by Talibs five months ago simply because he worked for the government.

"I am not going to be killed, Samira. This is a *jirga*."

"And you think they will support this American over their own?"

"It's a matter of honor. They are real Pashtuns. They will decide as they should."

She laughed, a little harshly. "Real Pashtuns. That's what you count on?" She rose, dusted her hand on her skirt, stepped back and examined him. "Do you know a single one of them personally?"

"My uncle is part of the *jirga*; I told you that."

"He is your mother's cousin. What do you know about him?"

"Samira, enough," Amin said gently. "If I am to be the father my children would look up to, I have to do this."

She lowered her voice and moved closer to him. "Oh, no, don't bring your children into this. Your impulse is as pure as a mud puddle, and you are only paying half attention to your own mind and heart, Amin, if you don't see that." He didn't answer, so she went on. "You're trying to change something that can't be changed anymore. Something I think could never have been changed by you alone, but in any case, that caravan moved on years ago. Why are the dogs still barking?"

He sighed and sank to his heels, squatting, so that he looked up at her as he spoke. He knew this would help soften her. "I could have done more back then," he said. "And yes, it troubles me still. But this is not related to that."

"Really? I think—do you want to know?"

He smiled. "If I didn't? Whatever is in your heart always rises to your tongue, Samira *jan*."

"You are being selfish in putting yourself in danger because of decades-old guilt. You're not thinking of your children at all."

He almost laughed at the courage it clearly took for her to say this. Theirs had been an arranged marriage; she was the daughter of his father's cousin, seven years younger than he. He'd found her beautiful, but so shy. They'd lived together in the States for two years while he studied, and then returned. Once back, she'd faced the criticism of her family, who thought Amin was misguided—or even immoral—to work with foreigners. Under these pressures, he'd observed her strength and confidence grow, and he loved her more profoundly than when they had first been married.

He rose. "Is this what you want to say to me in the moments before I leave?" he asked mildly.

"Our final conversation, you mean?" She glared at him.

"Samira, Allah is with me," Amin said. "But that is easier to achieve than gaining your support."

A weak smile appeared unbidden on her face, then vanished. "I see what you refuse to," she said.

"I see it," he said. "But I have to try. *Inshallah*, Mr. Todd will be freed, and I'll come back. *Inshallah*, in three days, this will be done. Now, give me something of your love to carry with me."

She stood silently for a moment, then went to the corner of the room, rummaged in a trunk, and returned with a piece of cloth he knew she'd cut from her wedding veil. He handed her his cup and put the cloth in a pocket inside his vest. He put his hand on her cheek, but she pulled away. "I am not ready to be a widow," she said. "My children are not ready to be fatherless."

"A few days, Samira." He smiled at her, gave her a wink. "And then I will be hungry, my wife. So be ready for my return."

Clarissa

September 12th

by the time Clarissa reaches the phone, it's gone dead. It rings again, almost immediately, and she lifts the receiver. Todd's voice, asking for something both urgent and vague. She calls his name and rushes to reply—*Wait, Todd, wait for me*—but then out of her mouth, instead of words, a river of color spills: yellow becoming orange becoming red, flowing away from her in an arc.

Clarissa awoke fevered, and fully, as if she'd just run a block, panting, with no tendrils left behind in the thick mud of lassitude. The call, Todd's voice, the colors: it felt like a memory but must have been a dream.

She turned on her side. Thursday morning, 2:53 a.m., if she believed the clock by her bed. More like noon, going by her own body. Which made some kind of sense: it was nearly 11:30 a.m. in Kabul, and she was living in two diametrically opposed time zones now. She flipped on the lights and glanced around the bedroom. Her possessions had begun to look strange to her, unfamiliar and unwelcome: an oblong tube of hand cream erect on the nightstand as if prepared to blast off and take flight, unread magazines lying fallen and limp, a closet with skirts clinging one to the next like timid sisters. None of it meant anything to her. Grief combined with fear had the force of a blizzard in the city, changing the shapes of buildings, turning the solid suddenly illusory, obscuring all dependable landmarks.

The only item she felt she needed—and even its practical use remained unclear—was a map of Afghanistan the FBI had given her; she'd posted it on the wall. Sometimes she stood close to it, becoming intimate with the country's geography: the terrain of regions, the location of provinces, the jumble of letters that made up the names of tiny villages. Sometimes she stood at a distance to study it, and the shape of Afghanistan became the profile of a woman gazing thoughtfully down at Pakistan, with Iran at her back and Turkmenistan, Tajikistan, and Uzbekistan on her head. What were these places? Except for Todd's presence, they meant nothing to her. She knew little of the terrain or the weather, and the towns were filled with strangers. Jack said they thought Todd was being held in Ghazni Province, right about where the woman's eye would be. A U.S. military presence remained in the province, but it was Taliban-held, Clarissa knew. Talibs had carried out assassinations of local officials as well as previous kidnappings, including the well-known abduction a few years back of twenty-three South Korean missionaries. After forty-two days, all but two were safely released. The other two: killed. Grim details; still, in certain moods, she found them comforting. As though mathematical odds could be extrapolated.

At this moment, however, nothing comforted. She went downstairs to the tiny room that was Todd's study, opened the door, and flipped on the lights. On the long desk sat a pile of yellow legal pads.

She picked one up to read Todd's scrawl. "Center expansion. Laura? Technical training—social media." In a corner on the floor, she saw three newsmagazines and a book spread at its spine, as if Todd had just put it down. *Seven Pillars of Wisdom* by T. E. Lawrence. Pinned to the wall above the light switch, a snapshot showed Todd, grinning, standing in the middle of a group of people. He'd told her the names of some, but Clarissa had met none of them. She felt sharply isolated. Who were they? How well did they know Todd? What would they tell Clarissa to do? What should she be doing?

Looking at the photo, she began to feel the walls squeeze in, an image from horror movies, she told herself. She sought a logical mind but could find no other way to classify the sensation. In the first days after the kidnapping, shock had made it seem as if her eyes were being tugged toward her temples. Then fear had left her stomach as raw as the inside of a carved pumpkin. But this new off-kilter reality—this sense that what had previously comforted her now threatened her—was something else, something she couldn't yet name. She found it hard to breathe, and even more, she was struck by the illogical certainty that if she didn't eject herself from her home, she might be crushed.

She'd never been given to insomnia before. She loved this two-story apartment that she and Todd had bought three years ago. On the rare occasions when she did awaken in the night, she'd found comfort in knowing she was safely cocooned in a place that felt, for the first time she could remember, like home. With all lights off, she could glide to the fridge, or find her way to her reading chair, or confidently locate the front-door handle to make sure it was locked. This home felt like an extension of self, a sanctuary.

Now, though, it seemed whatever turmoil waited on the city streets for a lone woman on foot was less dangerous than what hovered inside.

And if she was feeling trapped here in her sanctuary, how did Todd feel, confined in some place she struggled to imagine? She pictured a small compound, set apart from its neighbors and surrounded by high walls. Within, a building, the color of terra-cotta. She envisioned a thick but dusty rug on the floor along with a thinly padded mat for sleeping. One window, surely: the bit of blue sky a redemption. Any books? Probably not. A radio would also be too much to hope for. And the food? She wondered if he'd lost weight. He'd told her he had an iron stomach, which must be acting in his favor now, helping him stay physically strong. Emotionally, she imagined him solid, too, calm and confident. She didn't have it in her to imagine anything else.

Already wearing sweatpants and a T-shirt, she tied the laces to her tennis shoes, tugged a sweatshirt over her head, and slipped downstairs. Her stomach felt hollow. Hunger had largely left her during these last days—she'd always been an indifferent eater, but now she found herself forgetting about food altogether until she'd notice her hands were shaking. Ruby kept dropping off dishes, and Clarissa didn't have the heart to tell her to stop. Clarissa's kitchen had grown crowded, and she felt guilty having all that food around as if she were preparing for a party. Now, by the light of the refrigerator, she ate half a yogurt, putting the remainder back before going out the side door on the ground floor.

The air had fallen still, almost tranquil, something that happened only at night in the city and rarely even then. It felt crisp, but tempered by a bit of Indian summer. The streetlamp in front of her building spilled a murky teardrop on the sidewalk. To the left was the known neighborhood, to the right, less so. She hesitated only for a second, then turned right and began to walk, focusing on long strides, wanting to feel her body in motion, her arms swinging. Her sluggishness diminished with each step. At the corner, she headed toward Eastern Parkway, relatively well lit, and began to walk under the shadow of its paired trees, their kissing branches like a promise above her head.

She tried to relax as she walked. She wished she could think about something else for a while, but she couldn't, and now the previous day's conversation with the FBI ran through her mind. Jack on the speakerphone, Ruby, Mikey, Bill Snyder, and Clarissa sitting in her kitchen.

"One more contact," Jack had said at the start of the conversation, and she'd felt her breath catch in her throat—each "contact" felt hopeful and abrasive at once. The feds had a local guy speaking to the kidnappers separately, even as Amin tried his own path. To Clarissa, it seemed a little muddled, but Jack told her they didn't want to let this connection go unless Amin seemed to be making what he called "bankable progress."

"They repeated their demand for $1.5 million," Jack said. "They also said they'd like to speak directly to you, Clarissa."

"They asked for her by name?" Mikey asked.

"To his wife, they said. We told them we would check to see when that would be possible, and they are calling again this week, they said."

"What do they want with Clarissa?" Mikey's tone was protective.

"They aren't getting anywhere with our negotiators on the ransom request," Jack said. "We're stalling, and they get that. I think they've decided to go for the heart."

"Shouldn't your negotiators be more skillful?" Bill Snyder asked.

"*Should* I talk to them?" Clarissa interjected, not waiting for an answer to Bill's pointed but rhetorical question.

"Yes, I think you should," Jack said. "Right now they see Todd as goods. If they talk with you, they might begin to see him as human. We'd like to hook up your phone so the conversation can be recorded. We want you to say you want to achieve a solution and you want your husband home. Nothing else."

"Shouldn't she ask to talk directly to Todd?" Bill Snyder asked. "Wouldn't that be natural? Won't anything else sound phony?"

"Look." Jack sounded slightly impatient. "Let's run through where we are at this moment. From the three contacts we've had, we believe Todd is still in Afghanistan, and probably in the hands of criminals, as opposed to the Taliban."

"Of course our man on the ground has said that all along," Bill Snyder said. "So your guys are catching up to that viewpoint?"

"Well, the lines are blurry over there," Jack said. "Intel is cautious in making a call on this. But they note the kidnappers haven't issued any political demands, which kidnappers who solely identified with the Taliban likely would. This impacts the way we negotiate, and actually in a good way. It gives us a little more leverage. "

Bill Snyder gave an audible exasperated sigh. Clarissa hadn't warmed to Jack, either, but she decided she would talk to Bill privately later about adopting a more cooperative attitude, for Todd's sake.

"So ultimately we really have no idea who has Dad?" Ruby asked.

"They are terrorists," Jack said, "but we believe they're contingent terrorists, not absolute terrorists."

"Which means what?" Clarissa asked.

"They don't have much of a political agenda. It's about dollars. On the other hand, we've tried hard to talk down the dollar amount they're demanding, and they haven't budged at all. That concerns us."

"Why?" Ruby asked.

"If they're holding out so completely, they probably have a Plan B. And that likely involves selling Todd to the Taliban. The Taliban is aware of Todd's presence, obviously, and there's probably been some discussion of transfer of goods. Sorry, but remember, to them, this is business."

"We get that," Clarissa said.

"Right. So his situation is relatively stable at the moment, but if the kidnappers start to feel the monetary negotiations are irrevocably stalled . . ." He paused. "In that case, they would sell him—for less than they hope to get from us, but at least for something—to the Taliban or, even worse, specifically the Haqqani network. Haqqani's group is pretty intractable. Then your husband's situation becomes significantly worse. I can't stress that word enough. *Significantly*."

He didn't repeat aloud the question about permission to rescue, but Clarissa knew it dangled in the silent space on the phone line. She let her eyes linger over the faces in her kitchen. Ruby's position had not changed, and Bill continued to absolutely oppose military involvement. Mikey had told Clarissa privately that he thought if a military operation was to be attempted, it should be sooner rather than later, while Todd was physically stronger.

Why couldn't Clarissa simply say yes? Why did her gut keep saying no? Was that really what Todd would want?

On Eastern Parkway now, Clarissa passed a suitcase abandoned next to a bench, and then a parked car with a man sitting in front, dance-hall reggae blaring from his dashboard radio. "Givin ya mi man juice, jah mi baby madda, so we can passa-passa, oohman mi naa jesta." Indifferent to her destination, she cut in toward St. John's Place. She'd already left behind the few landmarks she knew from this neighborhood and was passing boarded-up brownstones and apartment buildings she didn't recognize.

As she walked, she tried to visualize Todd. He'd always made her think of the ocean. His tall, lanky body belonged to a lifeguard, but his eyes were long and fish-shaped, and his lips sprawled above his chin like they were lounging on a beach, enjoying themselves. His hair was graying but still brown, with a touch of gold from the sun. And his arms had always seemed surprisingly muscular; she'd teased him once that it was a shame they were so often hidden beneath shirtsleeves. His voice held a scratchy undertone, as though he were a smoker, though he wasn't.

She found herself remembering a trip they'd taken, right after they'd got married, to Tombstone in Arizona. Todd appreciated her interest in cemeteries, though he didn't share it. On this day, she'd done research and was ready to show him around the cemetery she'd never visited. Before she could, though, he'd taken her hand authoritatively, as if he knew where to go. He'd led her to a rock-covered grave marked with the epitaph they'd both laughingly read aloud in unison: "Here lies Lester Moore. Four slugs from a .44. No Les, no more."

She could recall with precision the heat of the sun and the dust of the cemetery, the ocotillo cacti and the spiny palo verde trees with their tiny, thirsty leaves. The feel of Todd's hand, warm but dry, as they wove between the tombstones. The closeness between them combined with the frivolity of the moment and the pleasure she'd taken in the fact that he'd brought her to the very grave site she'd intended to show him. It was as if they had communicated without words.

Why couldn't they communicate that way now?

An ice-cream truck passed, playing its repetitive tune. Too improbable to believe it patrolled the streets at this hour looking for ice-cream lovers; likely it was hawking something else. Clarissa stopped at that thought, wondering when she'd become so cynical, so convinced that little was as it appeared to be.

She glanced up at the street sign above her head: Ralph Avenue. She'd never had occasion to walk here before. The sidewalk was more littered than hers; the buildings presented themselves less gracefully. In front of one boarded-up door lay an empty Georgi vodka bottle. At the corner stood a bodega and a beauty salon, both sleeping behind metal shutters for the night. She paused, dropped her shoulders, and waited, listening to her own breath.

What do you want, Todd? Do I trust Amin? Do I tell Jack they can barge in with guns? I want this to end, I want you home. I want you alive. So give me a sign.

She stood motionless and waited, expectant, for several minutes. But nothing came, nothing at all, and quietly, adamantly, she cursed.

Danil

anil, crouching, paused in his work to watch an approaching woman halt and turn statue-like on a street corner in the dark half a block away. She didn't seem desperate, and she didn't act frightened or high. But it was all backward to see a woman alone in this neighborhood at this hour. If you did, she'd either be a crack whore yelling a waterfall of curses, or she'd be alert and nervous, head bowed, legs moving like a racetrack engine. In neither case would she gaze directly ahead, pausing as if to meditate, as if she were in some yoga studio in Brooklyn Heights.

Danil straightened and thought about calling out to her. Would it scare her to hear a voice emerging from the darkness? If she was sane, certainly yes. And if she wasn't, which was more likely, wouldn't he simply be starting shit for no good reason? Just last week, a man on a bicycle had paused at 3 a.m. and begun telling Danil a history of nearby Nostrand Avenue, which seemed potentially interesting until he started including details of the lives of the devils he said hid beneath the fire hydrants, cracking the sidewalks when they emerged in the afternoons. Danil finally had to pretend to be finished, walking once around the block, relieved to find the man gone when he returned a quarter of an hour later. No, thank you.

As he watched, considering his options, the woman seemed to shudder. She muttered something and then began walking again, passing without appearing to notice him, though near enough that he could have taken two steps forward and touched her. She was a bit over five feet tall with frizzy hair to her shoulders, slight in build, maybe in her late thirties. Her face was focused, but she didn't appear crazy or blurred by alcohol or drugs.

Again he thought about calling out, scolding, warning. *Hey, this is central Brooklyn. The economy sucks. Folks get desperate or crazed and then rub up right against other folks. What're you doing? Go home.*

People didn't realize how often they put themselves at risk, how many hundreds of times each week in ways both little and large. "Accidents" were nearly always, in retrospect, entirely predictable; that was one thing he'd learned at a cost, though not soon enough to teach his little brother. One simple mistake led to another, and then things spiraled out of control. The plane crash: preventable. The bicyclist hit by a car, the fire that starts in the fifth-floor apartment, Al Capone shooting himself in the groin. The soldier killed by friendly fire. There is an order in which things are broken, rules as quantifiable as gravity, if scientists would only turn their attention there. Within that order, logic dictated that some woman who chose to venture out onto the street on a blind-eyed, middle-of-the-night stroll could well be the city's next victim of violence.

Someone should warn her, this woman who didn't seem to understand.

As she moved away, he became caught in an airless moment of

142

doubt. Here he was, face-to-face with a question that had been nib-
bling at him for months. How much responsibility did one person
have toward another? If what you mainly had in common was being
alive at the same moment and in the same physical space, and then
being present enough to see a need, how far must your outstretched
hand reach?

Put another way: What did family, in the broadest sense, mean?

This interlocking of blood connections, this steady entity that traveled together over generations, linked by a sense of common history
and a mandate of loyalty—what happened when that history frayed,
interpretations of the past divided, loyalties unraveled? At that moment, wasn't it fair to rethink the narrowness of an obligation to those
who first tucked you in at night and revise the definition? Couldn't
Joni be his sister? Couldn't a woman on the street at night be his aunt?

And, in return, shouldn't someone else look after his own mother?

So here he was. His theory in practice. And his turn.

Who was he? Someone who helped, or not?

Then his mind swung the other direction. Only fifteen minutes
more, that was all he needed to finish up here, to complete the only
undertaking that brought him relief: this time, the face of a soldier
in a purple splotch of color. His more mature way of saying, *Fuck your
war*. See? He was growing up.

This woman wasn't in immediate trouble, as far as Danil could
tell. Besides, he had to watch out for himself. Out here, no one had
his back but him. He had to stay aware, cemented to his surroundings, and at the same time operate as if in a bubble, his energy focused on his work. It took effort to get into that space, and he wasn't
ready to move out of it yet.

But maybe this was the way it happened: one excuse after another to divert one's eyes, to let the stranger walk by. To pretend need didn't exist.

He took a deep breath and shuddered in an echo of the woman's tremor. Then he silenced his mind and turned back to the stencil on the wall: his loud whisper in the dark, a public intimacy, a swipe of spray paint that, remarkably, soothed like a lullaby.

Todd

September 12th

Y ou love your country?"

"Yes, I do," Todd said. "But I also love Afghanistan."

"Bah." Sher Agha made a scoffing sound. He'd arrived this morning, and, watching him through the window, Todd had become doubly certain he was in charge. It was in how Sher Agha held his shoulders back while talking to the other guards and in the way they leaned in toward him. He wore a white turban. Deep dimples sank into his cheeks. His face reminded Todd a little of Ahmad Shah Massoud's, only more worn, and his eyes did not contain the thoughtfulness of the famous murdered Northern Alliance commander's.

Todd sat uncomfortably in the middle of the room. His ribs were still painful. They'd also bound his ankles right after dawn prayers for no reason discernible to him, and that made it impossible for him to stand.

"Afghanistan," Sher Agha said, "is not one country. I am Pashtun. Your country makes patriots. People like you who think of themselves as American, without loyalty to the land of their grandfathers. But this does not make you open-minded. America does not produce humans. Humans would not behave as you have in Abu Ghraib, Guantánamo."

"I agree that was wrong. But it wasn't me."

"Yes," Sher Agha said, nodding as if with satisfaction. "And then you, all of you, deny responsibility. This is your pattern."

Todd opened his mouth to speak, but before he could, he heard, so clearly it almost seemed real, the voice of Amin. *Stay silent.*

"And even those of you who pretend to do good—to build schools," and here Sher Agha glared at Todd, "to help refugees—you are liars."

"I am not a liar." Again Amin's voice, more urgent. *Stay silent.* And in fact, Todd regretted his words as soon as he said them. They gave more power to this man; they legitimized the accusation. He shifted his weight slightly to the left but kept his gaze firm.

Sher Agha bent over and looked into Todd's face, as if examining an insect. "What is your religion? You are Jewish?"

"Raised Christian. But I am not practicing."

"So you are godless."

Say no. "No." Todd took a slow breath before continuing. He reminded himself of his long practice of pausing before breaking silence. "I believe," he said after a moment, "in one God who cares about us all. Who pays no attention to borders or ethnic differences."

Sher Agha straightened and ran his fingers into his dark beard. "But you don't personally worship this God? You don't want your own holy book?" He gave a short laugh, then added, "You do not feel that prayer will be useful to you now?"

"I pray," Todd said. "In my own way." *Say yes.* "But yes, thank you, I will take a copy of the Bible."

"Your own way." Sher Agha spit on the floor. "So does the heretic." He strode around the edges of the room, circling Todd once before turning to face him again. "You have no photograph of your wife?"

Todd met his gaze but did not answer. He did not want to talk about Clarissa. He was trying to hold her in a special place in his mind, apart from this situation, so that when he thought of her, it would feel like a sliver of freedom. He needed that now, and he didn't know for how long he would need it.

"But why not?" Sher Agha asked after a moment.

Todd laughed, a cracked sound he barely recognized. "Your men didn't offer me time to gather my belongings."

Sher Agha scoffed. "The foreigners I have met, they carry pictures of their wives. If they love them."

Should he ignore that remark or refute it? This all felt like some kind of complicated test that he was struggling through, doing poorly, and that would be crucial later.

Sher Agha shook his head. "So you are ready to take a new wife, then? Perhaps you dream of an Afghan woman?"

"I love my wife." Todd spoke each word distinctly. "I ask to speak with her, and to my daughter. I want to assure them that I'm all right."

"No one offered you that."

"But if you are humane, if you are so different from those who run Guantánamo, you will allow me a chance at least to reassure her."

In one seamless movement, Sher Agha pulled a knife from his voluminous clothing and began to wave it. "Don't talk to me," he began, his voice loud and ugly enough that Todd flinched, and then he slashed the knife toward Todd's leg, cutting his pants, slicing flesh, drawing immediate blood. "Do not talk to me about being humane." He drew back his arm as if to stab Todd, and then turned at the last second and threw the knife so that it lodged in the wall. "You do not know how lucky you are that it is me you deal with," he yelled. "But do not dare to use this language with me, after what you have done. You understand me?"

Against his will, Todd flashed on a stark image of a man whose head was being yanked back by the hair, his neck laid bare as if for a beheading. It passed in an instant, like a snapshot he'd glimpsed. He felt sick to his stomach, made small and hushed by this terrible new certainty: they did not see him as a person. They cared about him not at all. Eventually they would kill him.

After a minute he managed to raise his head to meet Sher Agha's glare directly. He could not speak, however. He knew if he tried, his voice might tremble. He felt the air thicken between them for what must have been a matter of seconds but felt like a quarter of an hour. Finally Sher Agha spit at the floor, and that seemed to release some of the tension.

Todd knew this captor held complete power over him in a practical sense. But he also knew he needed to pretend that wasn't the case, to reassert power of his own, even fictive power. He cleared his throat. "I need something to bandage my leg," he said. "And there is no need for me to be bound. Your guards are skilled; I can't escape. But this way, I also cannot use the bathroom."

Sher Agha studied him a moment. "Bah," he said. "Don't bother me with this. Your legs will be freed soon enough."

He turned as if to leave. "And my wife?" Todd asked, somehow wanting, needing now, to refer to Clari.

"Your wife," Sher Agha said. "*We* will talk to your wife. I hope for your sake, my friend, that she carries on her body a picture of you. That she loves you. Then perhaps she will work with us, and we will send you home."

"We do not have much money," Todd said carefully.

"Then we can sell you to those who care more about killing infidels than gaining money. Do you want that?"

Stay silent.

"Do you?" Sher Agha yelled so loudly that Todd recoiled again.

"No," he said.

"No. That's right. So you'd better hope your friends and your employer and your government will help your poor, moneyless wife." He walked to the door. "Bah. This conversation begins to bore me. I will have them bring you a Bible. It might be a good moment to find God."

Clarissa

September 12th

She had a rhythm going, and within that rhythm, her surroundings had vanished; she could have been anywhere: an alleyway in Venice, a hiking trail in the Swiss Alps, the Coney Island boardwalk. She walked without attention to where her feet landed, yet she noticed that one footstep sounded and felt unlike the other. This surprised her. The same set of legs, with their given shape and heft, were doing the stepping, a repetitive movement; still, each footfall seemed a unique moment, landing on a different piece of sidewalk or on the sidewalk differently. At the same time, within that diversity, a flow had developed now that she'd been walking for a while. Her energy had begun to run in a circular fashion from the ground, up one leg, to her belly, and back down the other leg, sweeping her forward rhythmically: *one, two; one, two; in, out; here we go*. A marching tune was what she imagined. She was marching in a tiny part of her city, and on an even tinier part of the Earth, in the middle of the night, as if nothing else of import existed. The world had shrunk, finally. No FBI, no Afghanistan, no warfare or impenetrable kidnappers speaking in a foreign tongue about an untenable topic, the terms for release of a husband. It had finally condensed to something she could manage.

How big did one's world need to be, anyway? There were people who spent their whole lives in one zip code, and then people who constantly fled for new adventures, horizons, and faces. She and Todd had had two different reactions to life's losses, and it had created opposing desires that they'd never really discussed: in her, the belief in putting down roots to create meaning, and in him, the hunt for meaning in distant alleys beyond the boundaries of home.

And now the differences were magnified. Now Todd was held prisoner on soil stained by decades of bloodshed, in a part of the planet that had felt to him almost like a second home and seemed to her so unlikely as to be imaginary.

Todd had known, at least academically, the risks he took. He'd even, on some level, embraced them. It was part of how he looked at life: nothing mundane, thank you. Everything writ large. She had realized even before they married that Todd would never have the patience for aging: little aches and pains that developed into larger vulnerabilities, flipping through women's magazines in doctors' offices, a morning marked by its regimen of medicines. He once told her he would not want to live long and go peacefully if that meant settling at some tottering age in some vacation home on a picturesque, boring lake; *God, kill me first*, he'd said.

She'd been walking for two hours in what turned out to be a large and uneven circle, and now she was about twenty minutes from home. Beneath a tall streetlight, Clarissa saw a figure painted on a cement overpass wall. She paused; she'd never noticed it before.

Below her feet ran the S train, a boring dinner partner, touching down at five stops before doing it all over again, back and forth, its monotonous life so tightly contained. At this hour, the track yawned empty, trains moving sleepily, so she had museum-silence to examine the woman kneeling with her hands in her lap. Her skirt, an American flag, mushroomed around her. On her head sat a bird, painted red, claws tangled in her hair, wings spread as though about to take flight. But it was her expression that particularly caught Clarissa's attention. She had a closed face, like a passport inspector, as if she didn't care what you thought of her; her job was to decide what she thought of you.

Clarissa looked again at the bird. Was this an image of her and Todd, she kneeling, Todd ready to fly? Could street art over a shuttle track be articulating their barely spoken argument?

More likely this was all just predawn, sleep-deprived nonsense, the clarifying effect of crisp night air offset by the fact that this wasn't—or hadn't been, until lately—her usual hour to be awake.

She leaned over to look once more and saw four letters that made her catch her breath: "Afgh."

"You like it?"

She startled at the sound of a male voice near at hand, straightened, and turned to look into wide green eyes. Where had he come from? She recalled in an instant that she stood only four blocks from the armory, with its mandated around-the-clock police presence. It housed the city's roughest men outside prison, those halfway between freedom and captivity with nowhere to go and little motivation to avoid crimes they'd already practiced, though not quite yet perfected, in an alleyway in the Bronx or up a fire escape in Manhattan. Outcasts living in testosterone-filled bunk beds with mornings, she imagined, of mold-cornered showers and bruised bananas, yesterday's shirt, and too few plans.

There was no graying in the sky, no comfort in the sense that dawn was nearly there or even that daylight had ever existed. She'd looked at her cell phone a few minutes ago, so she knew it was about 4:40 a.m., which might be a detail to remember later for the police.

And then she took in more of the man himself. Maybe his late twenties, early thirties, thin, fit, wearing a backpack. Jeans with a rip in the thigh, the material held together with two large safety pins. Clean-shaven with mussed hair and hands that looked stained by something. But he was clear-eyed. That was key. Because of that, she didn't run. She did back up.

"I only wondered," he said after a moment. "Because it's mine."

"*Yours?*" Clarissa hadn't intended to speak, but the absurdity of his claiming a painting sprayed on a cement wall forced her words.

The man laughed. "I mean I did it. See?"

Embarrassed that she hadn't understood at first, Clarissa looked where he pointed his flashlight, the edge of the woman's skirt. She saw four letters: IMOP.

"Yeah," he said, as though she'd asked a question. "That's how I sign them."

"That's your name?" she asked, doubt threaded in her words.

"No. My tag."

"I-mop," she said, thinking it sounded like a cleaning product. "What does it mean?"

He shrugged. "Just my tag."

She pointed to the letters "Afgh." "And what does that mean?"

"Afghanistan," he said.

Even though that had been her first thought, she was shocked to have it confirmed, and in such a matter-of-fact way. And then she wondered: Was he telling the truth? People lied more in the dark, as though the shadows gave them permission.

"Why does it say 'Afghanistan'?" she asked.

He paused, taking in her face. "Just does."

"I . . . I have a connection to the country, and so I wondered . . ."

"Yeah?" he said, his eyes still wary. "It's a fucked-up place."

A block away, a car alarm sounded. She started, the way she did in the morning when her alarm clock went off. Only then did she realize this might be about when she would be waking up, in her regular, former life. Only then did she begin to feel tired.

"I'm Clarissa," she said.

"Danil," he answered after a moment.

"You live around here?"

"Around." He took a step away from her, preparing to go.

"My husband." She spoke quickly. "He works with refugees. He was kidnapped. In Afghanistan a few days ago. He's being held there now. We aren't supposed to talk about it, so my friends don't even know. But that's why I—why I was asking. I just wondered . . ."

She felt him examining her again, maybe wondering whether *she* could be believed. "That's rough," he said after a minute. He looked off into a dark horizon and then back at her. "My brother was in Afghanistan," he said. "First Battalion, 32nd Infantry, 10th Mountain Division."

She stared at him, willing him to go on. "He's back home now?" she asked after a moment.

He shook his head. "Didn't make it."

"Oh." She released a breath. "I'm sorry."

"Yeah." He gestured with his head to the painting on the wall. "This is for him. Or I guess it's for me, but because of him."

Unlike the face of the woman he'd painted, his was open. Clarissa hesitated, then spoke without censoring herself. "You know, my stepdaughter keeps making me food—way too much of it. I live a few blocks away. You want something to eat? An early breakfast? You'd be doing me a favor if . . ."

He held up one hand, shaking his head, but she kept talking.

"I mean, it's not exactly breakfast food," she said. "But then, it's not quite breakfast time when you've been up all night. And she's a professional chef, so I know it's good and . . . and it's kind of driving me crazy. I can't throw it out, but I absolutely can't eat it all."

Still slightly shaking his head, he stared at her, then rubbed the back of his neck. It was an old man's gesture; it surprised her. What was she doing inviting him to her home? What was she thinking; who had she become?

"I'm sorry, that sounded weird," she said. "It *is* weird. It's a weird time for me. Never mind."

"Sure," he said.

"What?"

He gave an odd half-smile. "Why not? I haven't had anything since a pizza slice for yesterday's lunch, and the paint fumes left me hungry."

Now that he'd said yes, she suddenly felt awkward. "So, well, okay . . ."

"Are *you* hungry?" he asked.

She paused. "Yes, actually. I am."

"So let's go have the un-breakfast," he said, as if it had been his proposal all along. "Let's go eat your worry food."

"You mean comfort food?"

"The food nice people make to try to take away your fears. Only that never happens if you eat it alone."

She smiled. "Right. So, okay, then. Follow me." And despite the hours she'd spent awake, she felt a rush of energy that surprised her, and a flash of optimism—brief but welcome—that she hadn't felt since the day Todd had been taken.

Mandy

September 12th

So how's Jimmy?"

In the computer room in the guesthouse, Mandy started. She'd hung up on Skype with her son five minutes earlier and hadn't moved since then, thinking over the conversation—or mostly the silences, the words unspoken.

"Is it just me," she asked, "or are you exceptionally talented in sneaking up on someone?"

Hammon laughed and handed her a glass. "It's part of the job description, isn't it? Here's some fresh lemonade. Rumi made it. It's delicious." He sat down on a worn couch.

"Thanks," she said. "And thanks for not telling Jimmy about the kidnapping."

Hammon shrugged. "It's what we do."

"I get that. And so does he, of course, which is why he has the sense there's something I'm not telling him." She laughed. "I always had that sense, too, when he was here."

"And he probably worries even more than you did, since he's seen how it can go down here," Hammon said.

Mandy sipped the lemonade. She'd been thinking a lot about Jimmy. He was always at the edges of her mind at home, too, but it felt different here. She had time, she had distance, and she was often alone. In that space, she'd made a disturbing discovery.

She was an emergency-room nurse, and besides that a mother, and nurturing should come naturally where Jimmy was involved, but the emotion she'd been fighting and barely burying had been anger, pure and strong. In fact, she'd been repressing anger toward Jimmy for months now—for getting hurt in the war, but not exactly that. More precisely, for not getting better, for not finding a way to make things work again so that they could go on—maybe not as before, exactly, but go on. He was the one who'd lost his legs, the left below the knee and the right at the thigh. And still she was fuming: that he'd made the choice to go to war; that he'd gotten badly hurt, and now the rest of everything that followed would be changed. Nothing would ever feel to her wholly safe again. She could never return to the softness of that time when Jimmy had been a baby in her arms and her life had felt full of possibilities. Or even to the promise of the time before the war, when she'd imagined him a father playing football with his kids on the lawn while she and a daughter-in-law she loved put the finishing touches on a big dinner. She was mad, too, that all around her, the message she heard was that she should just feel grateful that Jimmy was alive.

And so even as she'd been taking care of him—feeding him, helping him bathe, giving him pep talks, meeting with his doctors—surely, on some level, he'd felt the underlying foundation of her suffocated fury. He'd probably recognized it before she had. Worse, it had to contribute to his own anger and bitterness.

So now, on top of newly recognized anger, she felt deeply ashamed.

"It *is* good lemonade," Mandy said, breaking the silence that Hammon was so good at keeping.

"That Rumi, he's something," Hammon said. "How's the work been going?" he asked after a moment.

Mandy nodded. "Good. Fine." Then she shrugged. "Actually, I don't know. They're happy to have the supplies I bring, and they listen in a friendly way while I explain ways to improve patient care. But I don't have the sense that they'll follow through at all. I leave illustrated instructions, and I think they throw the sheets away the minute I'm out the door."

Hammon laughed. "Well, there's probably some of that, but you may be having a bigger impact than you realize."

"I'm not sure. Yesterday at the center for addicts, the director pulled me aside and told me not to be so public with the fact that I'm American."

Hammon's face grew more serious. "What was her tone?"

"I don't know. One of her assistants translated."

"What did you say?"

"I asked why. The assistant didn't even repeat that question to the director. She told me the director's husband was visiting family up north when he and his father were killed during an American night raid. 'Collateral damage,' she called it. Her English was good enough for that phrase."

Hammon sighed.

"I told the director I was sorry, and I hugged her. She hugged me back, and the assistant hugged me, too, but then she repeated again— don't tell anyone I'm American. Better to say I'm German."

Hammon's face softened into a smile. "German, huh? So what are you going to do?"

" 'Sauerkraut.' That's the single word I can say in German. I'm only going to get caught lying if I try that."

He nodded. "It would be better just to go unnoticed. On the streets, keep your head down and don't talk. You should be fine inside the hospitals, but for the refugee camps, a couple of my guys are going with you."

Mandy took a sip of the lemonade. "I have to tell you," she said, "even with the director's warning, I really don't feel in danger."

"No one ever does. It's Kabul, not the front line: that's what everyone thinks when they first get here. After a while, they realize the front line is fluid. It's everywhere."

"How long have you been in this work, Hammon?"

"Long time," he said.

"Being vague about your personal details again?"

He smiled. "A professional habit, I guess. You get used to revealing nothing." He rolled his shoulders. "Truth is, I was a big disappointment to my mom."

"You? How so?"

"She wanted me to be a chess player."

"*What?*" Mandy smiled.

"I was really good at chess, back in school. She couldn't understand when I began working out and then joined the military. And now, of course, this."

"Well, from chess player to this: that's a journey."

"I don't know. I often think I play a form of chess as part of my job, actually." Hammon rubbed his stubble-covered chin. "Still, my mom was disappointed. It wasn't how she'd imagined the future."

Mandy studied Hammon's face. When he spoke, it was with purpose. "Did she get over it?" she asked after a moment.

Hammon rose to his feet. "She did. But not without effort. She said it required that she take all her clothes to the charity shop."

"What do you mean?"

Hammon laughed at Mandy's puzzled face. "She had this saying. When she had to rethink things, she called it taking everything to the charity shop. So that she had a clean closet and could be ready for new outfits, symbolically speaking." He paused. "You see?"

Mandy leaned back in her chair. "Yes," she said. "I think I do."

Hammon gave her a short wave. "See you at dinner." And then he backed out as silently as he'd entered, leaving Mandy to her thoughts.

Danil

danil followed the woman Clarissa into her home. She didn't pause to unlock her door; she'd clearly left it unbolted when she'd gone out in the dark. He found that he liked this act of trust, even if it was actually inattention or eccentricity. Most people protected what didn't need protecting, he'd come to believe, and were too casual with what was important. He'd been that way too once.

She led him into the kitchen. "Sit down," she said, and he did, stretching his legs out beneath the table; he was accustomed to making himself at home in unfamiliar places. He thought of it as one of his gifts: this ability to fit in, to one degree or another.

"What can I get you? We have lots of pasta salad, and there is a chicken casserole, and something with broccoli and cauliflower, and fresh bread."

"Any of it sounds good," he said, taking in the kitchen, which was large—as big as the combined space of his own kitchen, living room, and dining room. It was neater, too, and the honey-colored wood made it feel warm.

"How about a little of everything?" she said as she reached into the pantry and pulled out a plate. She went to the refrigerator and began removing containers. The fridge was full; he could see she hadn't been kidding about that.

"So," Clarissa said as she put a plate in front of him with chicken and a serving of pasta, basil, and zucchini. "How long have you been doing street art?"

"About four years," he said.

She ground some coffee beans and spooned them into a filter. "Are a lot of them about Afghanistan?"

"In one way or another, yeah. I only started—I started after." He paused. "Pasta salad is great. Your daughter's a good cook."

"Stepdaughter. Yes, isn't she?" Clarissa sat across from Danil and watched him eat. "Do you live in the neighborhood?"

"Over on Bergen," he said.

"And what do you do? I mean, besides the street art?"

He laughed slightly. "Hardly seems enough, does it?"

"I didn't mean it that way," she said. "How do you take your coffee?"

"Black," he said, and watched as she rose and poured him a cup. "I got a BA from Ohio University. Then I moved to New York. I went to Pratt for a year. Wasn't for me. Now I paint the interiors of people's homes, or the interiors of apartments or offices between occupants."

"Pays the rent, I'd imagine."

He shrugged. "I suppose it does."

"Not easy making it as an artist."

Danil made a scoffing sound. "I hate that word."

"Why?"

"All I'm doing out there is remembering my brother. I'm just . . ." He shrugged. "You know, I saw you pass by earlier, and I thought you were crazy, or a crackhead, or something."

"Yeah? Why?"

"Out at that hour, muttering to yourself." He couldn't quite confess that he'd considered, and rejected, the idea of asking if she needed help.

"That does sound a bit crazy." She softly drummed her fingers on the tabletop for a moment. "I couldn't sleep," she said. "I can't sleep."

He studied her a moment. "Yes, now I get that."

"If you don't mind . . . What happened to your brother?"

Danil looked out the kitchen window. She was direct, this lady. But he couldn't go there. "You know, I'm sorry, I really don't want to talk—"

"No, I understand," she said. "I don't want people asking me too many questions either. I'm just—" She spread her hands. "I spent the last couple years trying to ignore Afghanistan, the whole region. We've only been married three years, and I wanted my husband to come home. He was supposed to, after this rotation. But even so, I—I was angry with him for staying over there. On some level, I didn't want to know anything about the place. But now?" She shook her head.

He studied her a minute. He knew this phase, this drive to make sense of chaos, to understand. He'd felt it, too, once. He ate another bite. "So how long has your husband worked over there?"

"In the region, off and on, for about five years."

"Long time."

"Long enough." Abruptly, she stood up. "I'll be right back."

She returned with a laptop. "I found this map online the other night." She clicked on a web page. "Here's Ghazni. That's where they say my husband is being held. When they told me that, I thought, *Good! Something definite.* But what does it actually mean? If you scroll in, look. Ghazni turns into all these little towns. He might be held in Ramak, or Lowy Shar, or even closer to the Tribal Areas." She shook her head. "I'm trying to imagine him. I'm trying to feel what it must be like. But it's so remote, you know? And when I search for Ghazni, looking for images, the first thing that comes up are women in burqas who've been killed."

She slid the laptop over to him. He repositioned the map on the screen and scrolled into the ranges of the Hindu Kush as they reached toward the border with Pakistan. "My brother was stationed in a place that doesn't have a name. It was in this area north of Jalalabad. Pech Valley."

"Yes, I've heard of it," she said.

"There's a river, and a village called Nangalam."

"I've seen it on the map," she said, and her voice sounded excited.

"It must have been a good map because it's not on most. It's barely a town. Forty or fifty houses. A few restaurants—my brother called them 'choke-and-pukes.' A couple shops for the locals. That's it. And once you put the town at your back, you're immediately in the mountains that press up against Nangalam. That's where my brother was based. It was his training. His unit specialized in mountain combat. But he said there was no way to understand how sheer the drops were unless you'd seen them. It's ghost-land, he said—a man with a gun walking in those mountains disappears into the shadows. A few houses are scattered around on tiny rock outcroppings, lone rangers. They aren't part of any system at all. My brother told me in a letter once, 'For all intents and purposes, this place does not exist.' "

"The badlands of Afghanistan."

"The people who live there," Danil agreed, "are tough, tougher than we can imagine. And they don't want to see outsiders. Not even Afghan outsiders, certainly not American outsiders." He leaned back in his chair. "My brother had a girlfriend and a job, but he thought leaving that behind to go to Afghanistan was important. He said he wanted to make the world safer for their kids. What a cliché—but he believed it. He even loved it, the training, at least. He'd never been involved in anything like that before. I told him he was crazy. I told him that repeatedly. After he got there and wrote me letters describing what he was seeing, I began to think about the whole setup. It doesn't make any sense for us to be there. It's an impossible mission, even with special training. How, in this impenetrable place, can we hope to accomplish anything—except take life and give it up?"

Clarissa smiled at him, a little sadly. "My husband believes in connections between cultures, among strangers. He believes in progress and that he's accomplished things."

"No disrespect," he said. "My brother's perspective was a little off-kilter while he was over there, too. What he told me was that being there gave his life 'clarity.' Sure, I understand, you have someone giving you orders, you don't have to face the fear of figuring things out for yourself. But in terms of helping, in terms of solving anything—it's all too fucked up."

"My husband would say work like his helps make it better, and that we can't do what we've done in that country and then simply turn our backs on them."

"We can if the alternative only makes it worse," Danil said, adding, "Sorry."

She shrugged. "I'm not sure what I believe, and I'm not sure what my husband would say now."

"I flew to Kabul after Piotr was killed," Danil said. "I wanted to talk to the military. I wanted to go directly to his FOB—Forward Operating Base—but they wouldn't let me. Instead the commander of his unit flew in to see me. He came to Bagram, and they took me there."

"What did he tell you?"

"Some shit," Danil said. He couldn't share that.

"Did it help?"

He half laughed. "I'm alone. My brother's not coming back. So, hell, no." Then he stopped. He'd said more than he'd meant to already.

She waited for a moment. "There's nothing to fill that space, is there?"

"Nothing." Danil practically spit the word. "You get more used to it, but the gap doesn't disappear. What I really thought after talking to the commander was that all these words, a flood of them, miss the point. My brother died. For what? And now the path of my life has been fucked up." His voice, he realized, had grown loud. He cleared his throat. "Sorry," he repeated.

"No, this is how I feel, too," she said. She hesitated a moment, then reached out and touched the back of his hand with her fingers. "I'd like to see your work."

"Sure," he said. "Sometime . . ."

"No, I mean now." She withdrew her hand and brought it to her neck. "I can drive us around."

He studied her, trying to decide if she was serious.

"I'd like to see," she hesitated, "what you've done."

"Aren't you tired?"

"Not really. You?"

She wasn't high; she wasn't crazy. She was in trouble; he could feel that, see that. He pulled his hands onto his lap and looked down at them, then up at her. "Okay," he said. "Sure. We can do that."

She smiled and rose. "I'll be right back." He watched her leave the kitchen and heard her climb the stairs to the second floor.

The house felt quiet, unlike his apartment with its paper-thin walls. All the street noises seemed far away. He was, he realized, suddenly very tired of words. He wouldn't be able to talk much more. He'd go get his camera, and he'd give her directions, and he'd take the pictures of the work, and she'd have to be okay with that. It would have to be help enough.

He took one more sip of coffee. On the laptop, he zoomed in on the map and switched to satellite view. He watched as it turned the Pech River into an ugly scar tattooing the hostile terrain that had been home for the 1st Battalion, 32nd Infantry, 10th Mountain Division, and the place his brother had died.

Clarissa

P ull over," Danil said, gesturing with his head. "I'll be a minute."

He hopped out and darted across the street to a narrow, unnumbered building four stories high, crowded next to a tiny single-level shop as if it were a protective big brother. "Johnny's Variety Deli Convenience," read the sign above the store. "Sweat Suits Men's Shoes Cold Beer Cigarettes Snacks." A white T-shirt hung in front like a signal of surrender. The building looked run-down from the outside; three separate locks defended the front door. Danil pulled out a set of keys, looked back at her and waved, and then shot through the door.

Clarissa was probably crazy—no, she was crazy, driving around to look at graffiti with someone she'd met a few hours ago. Because, what? Because he, like her, had a troubled connection to Afghanistan? But everything felt out of control, anyway, and she felt drawn to Danil, something about his face—his unusual green eyes. But more than that. To her he looked older than he said he was, closer to her own age with lines already etched on his forehead, maybe because he'd already gone through the worst. She wanted to know him, to understand how he'd come out on the other side. She wanted, too, someone she could talk to about this without all the emotional tension and history that came with every conversation with Ruby, with Mikey.

Danil emerged from the building, held his camera aloft, and got into the passenger seat. "We'll stay around here," he said. "I've done the odd piece in Manhattan or Queens, but most of the work is nearby."

He directed her a few streets away and then told her to pull over. She followed him on foot halfway up the block. On a second-story wall set back from the street, she saw it. A soldier's face, about five feet wide, his head tilted to one side and his eyes closed, sleeping or meditating or dead. His skin seemed almost to glow. "IMOP," it said in a corner, along with "Afgh."

"How do you do it?"

"Different ways." He snapped a few pictures as he spoke. "Sometimes I use photos, or compilations of photos. Sometimes I draw it. Then I use an old overhead projector to make it larger. I trace it and cut layers out of a piece of paper or, when I can afford it, plastic acetate. After that, it's all the power of a can, or two or three, of spray paint. When I'm finished, I hand it over to the wind, the rain, people on the street."

"And this one?"

"My brother's face," he said, and turned back toward the car, severing the conversation. She took one last look before following.

They had to park a couple of blocks from the next stencil. Standing six feet tall on a corner near the metal back door of a Mexican restaurant, it showed a uniformed American soldier striding forward, trying to unfasten his fire-engulfed helmet. Flames also surged from his shoulders.

Danil took photos silently, and they headed back to the car. She felt oddly gratified to see that he was talented. She studied him a moment, imagining him working in front of this door in the middle of some night.

"Urban history," she said in the car. "This is part of it, and it's the only history that still feels alive to me. I love it. When I started college, I thought I wanted to be an urban activist."

"A what?"

"Yeah." She laughed. "They didn't offer that major. But what I wanted was to bring communities together within the urban environment in unexpected ways. In the 1970s in Austria, people strapped on wood frames that took up the same amount of space as a car and then took to the streets. It was a protest against the alienation that cars encourage, and at the same time, it created new conversations, new alliances. Anyway, maybe that's kind of what street art is now."

"Urban activist."

"No money in it, of course." She laughed again.

"Never is, is there, in what we want to do most?"

"Sometimes there is," she said. "When we're very lucky. When things align perfectly." She felt him looking at her and turned toward him. "What?" she said.

He hesitated a moment. "Turn left up here," he said. And then after a minute: "Two more blocks. Right-hand side. Over there."

The next piece, on a whitewashed wall, showed a soldier lying in a splotch of red and another soldier walking away, through a door. It was dramatic but hard. She found herself thinking of rescue attempts.

"Left, then right. One more block and on the left-hand side."

This one showed an Islamic woman wearing a headscarf and kneeling, an expression of anguish on her face, her arms spread open, one hand colored red. Someone had painted a tag, the letters "KBZ," on her knee. She wanted to ask him about it, but he turned away before she could.

"Four blocks and then a right. Okay, left there. Park anywhere."

This one: a woman cradling a limp child, her mouth opened.

"Two blocks and then a right and then a left for three blocks."

She followed him to a brick wall covered with graffiti. In one corner stood a piece she, by now, recognized immediately as his. It showed a shadow of a male form, and where the figure casting the shadow would be standing, Danil had painted flames. The same insignia: "IMOP" and "Afgh."

This one, against her will, brought tears. It was, she knew, the cumulative impact of the images, her fears for Todd, and the lack of sleep. Not wanting Danil to see, she turned away, but too late; he'd already noticed. He stepped closer. "You okay?"

She managed to smile. "You must think I'm completely unbalanced."

He shook his head. "Tired. And stressed. And afraid."

"This isn't me at my best."

"You seem to be doing fine, given the circumstances. But maybe that's enough for now."

She did, suddenly, feel exhausted. She glanced at her watch and inhaled sharply. "Oh, God. I'm supposed to be on a speakerphone with the FBI in twenty minutes. I'm going to drive right back to my place, okay? Let you out there."

"Sure."

They both got in the car quickly. "I want to thank you for this." She glanced at him.

He didn't meet her gaze; he was looking down at his camera. "Sure," he said.

She started the car and pulled into the street. "You know where I live. Come by anytime for worry food."

He looked up then and smiled. "I will."

And with those words she felt a sudden, unexpected longing that surprised her—a longing for forbidden conversation of the sort that she might have had before with Todd, this time about Afghanistan, about her husband, about loss and fear and endless nights.

Jirga

Amin

September 13th

everything was mostly in place by the time he arrived. The plentiful food his uncle's family had provided for the participants was displayed beneath the shade of a tarp. Nearby, a deep red carpet suffocated the bald earth, and many already sat at its border. Several glanced his direction; none smiled. Amin lingered outside the circle, waiting for his uncle Mahyar to emerge from a group of half-a-dozen men who stood off to one side. Mahyar effusively kissed Amin's cheeks, took his hand, sent greetings to his mother. Only when he pulled Amin to the side did his expression turn dark.

"You have put us both in jeopardy, Amin," he said, speaking quietly, quickly.

"I'm sorry for that."

Mahyar waved his hand dismissively. "Listen. I haven't much time. Be careful what you press for. The elders must be sure the other side will accept any decision they reach. Otherwise they risk dishonor. This is their limitation. So look for a compromise."

"Compromise, uncle?"

"I've done everything I can to lay the ground for you. But it's a complicated game you are here to play, my son. For my sake and yours, be skilled. If you have a way out for all sides, offer it."

"He must be freed. What compromise is possible? He's not—"

His uncle shook his head, cutting Amin off. "We speak now of strategy. I live among these men. So hear me. If you have no planned compromise, listen for theirs. It will not come directly from an elder. When it comes, however, do not reject it, Amin."

He abruptly moved away, smiling in a way that felt artificial and pointless and necessary all at once. Amin understood that further discussion would arouse unwelcome attention. "Thank you, uncle," Amin called after him. "I will carry your greetings to our family." Then he paused, nodding to a few of the elders before approaching the circle, finding an opening, and dropping himself to a seated position. He knew he was being stared at, but as a guest and an outsider, it was improper for him to stare back. Still, he tried to surreptitiously evaluate the attendees. Beyond the inner circle, which he had joined, was a second loop of those who by tradition would not speak but were there to observe.

He felt sure the kidnappers had someone representing them here, or were here themselves, and that the elders, and perhaps even his uncle, knew who they were; he wondered if they were in the inner ring or the secondary one, and if he would hear from them directly or through a proxy, and if he would be able to discern the difference. He was certain that many men who would never carry out a kidnapping nevertheless thought poorly of him for his presence here and the nature of his appeal and might well want to express their disdain.

The session was called to order with a brief prayer. Then Amin was introduced by the name of his father to stress to everyone here that he, too, was Pashtun. The meeting, he knew, would not be run by any one man; instead it would operate on the basis of perceived equality. Two of the elders had small piles of stones in front of them that they would use in judging the arguments. One of these two nodded at him, a signal that he was to present his case, though of course everyone present already knew why he was here.

Amin began by describing Todd's work over the several years he'd been coming to Afghanistan. While he spoke, each of the two elders moved their rocks around as if taking notes. "This man was in this country to help, and as a guest." Amin paused. "I know I need not tell you this action of forcibly holding him violates the rules by which we honorably treat guests. You know—"

"But he is not only a guest, is he?" one of the men in the circle interrupted. He looked about forty years old, with a white turban and dark eyes that seemed at once unfocused and angry.

Amin ignored the interruption. "I come to you for help because from Kabul, where he was taken, he was driven to this province on the first day."

"You don't know that he's still here," said one of the stone-moving elders.

"That's correct," Amin conceded. "He has not been allowed contact with anyone. But those who took him are connected here, even if they've moved elsewhere. He has dependents, a wife and a daughter, and no male members in his immediate family. So for their sake also, I ask your help in locating him—today—and securing his immediate release."

"Today?" the elder said. "You've lost the Afghan's patience if you make such a request. It would be difficult to fulfill your application within a month, not to speak of a single moon."

"Respectfully, I know the honored members of this *jirga* can draw camel milk from stones before sundown if they view it as correct and necessary," Amin said.

There came an appreciative titter from the second circle, but a stern expression remained bitten into the elder's face.

Then a graybeard who had not yet spoken cleared his throat. "Can you tell us what this patron of yours believed to be his mission in our country?" he asked.

"His job is to help refugees," Amin said solidly. "Pashtun and others. As our refugees are, for a time, citizens of the world, so has this man been welcomed here as a temporary citizen of Afghanistan."

"Still, he moved beyond these parameters," the graybeard continued.

"We have heard," added another man in the circle, "that he meddles in affairs that have nothing to do with refugees. Affairs that he doesn't understand."

"No," Amin said. "That information is wrong."

"He entices our women to act as Western women," the man continued. "He corrupts them."

"No," Amin said.

"These foreigners think they can tell us how to be men?" This again from the angry-looking man. "Our women are our jewels. We know how to care for them—as well as for our own refugees." An elder turned toward the speaker with lowered eyelids, as though to silence him.

Zarlasht. Amin still didn't fully understand her motives, but he grew more certain in that moment that she'd played a role, even if unwittingly. Maybe someone had learned that she was appealing to Todd. Maybe she'd given him up in return for safety for her or her daughter. He might never know. He didn't have time to puzzle it out now. They waited for him to respond, and by tone and demeanor, he had to make it clear that he had nothing to hide.

"He cannot control who visits his office or what requests are made of him," Amin said. "But I am certain his involvement in Afghanistan has been limited to the refugees. Any other perception is . . ." He hesitated. He wanted to say a lie. But perhaps this was a form of compromise he could make. "Is a misunderstanding," he said. "This man is a victim. I know this *jirga* would not sully its place among our people by supporting criminal acts. This is not doing Pashtu. Our collective honor is at stake."

"Our honor? *Our* people?" A man sitting two places away from the angry man spoke now. His voice, though loud, held no emotion. "What our people need, cousin, is money. Call it ransom, call it a salary—*you* are already getting money from the foreigners. Why shouldn't we?"

Amin looked at the speaker, who quietly stroked his beard as he spoke, as if meditating on an interpretation of the Quran. Amin was at a disadvantage not knowing these men or their backgrounds, but he wondered if the speaker had unwittingly revealed more than he intended. " 'We'?" he asked.

"I speak theoretically, of course," the man answered, confident, even arrogant.

"It's true," another man said. "They pour money into here in the billions. But it's written on the lines of our faces that we've seen not an Af. What would it hurt for some of the money that you grab in Kabul to make its way here?"

One of the elders with the rocks moved two of them into different places, an impenetrable shorthand recorded on the earth.

"To gain money in this way is dishonorable," Amin said.

"Nor have they been honorable, these Americans," the man countered.

There was murmuring then, agreement on this issue. Even without the ability to decipher the meaning of the piles of stones, Amin understood that he needed to alter the direction of the conversation. He remembered his argument with Najib all those years ago, and the moment when he knew it had become unwinnable. He would not fail a second time. Before he could speak, though, one of the graybeards did.

"We do not side with criminals, whatever their motivation," the elder said, his voice clear, his tone scolding as though to stop a pointless quarrel. The circle silenced to allow him to finish. "But I must make it clear. We view the Americans as criminals as well."

"Here is my word," Amin said. "This man is not a criminal."

"Your opinion on who is or is not a criminal," the angry man said, "has already in the past proven to be false."

"Enough of your talking," another man said over him.

The jumble of voices signaled the breakdown of the process. "Wait," Amin said, trying to wrestle back attention, but his uncle rose and took his arm.

"It's time to go," he said.

"But uncle—" Amin couldn't leave like this. Not again.

"Do not argue." His uncle pulled him to his feet, eliminating the possibility of choice. "Come now."

part three

The year before I die I'll send out

four hymns to track down God.

But it starts here.

A song about what is near.

What is near.

The battlefield within us

Where we, the Bones of the Dead,

fight to become living.

— TOMAS TRANSTROMER

We've lost the knack of living in the

world with the sensation of safety.

— MAURICE SENDAK, AUTHOR

OF *WHERE THE WILD*

THINGS ARE

Najibullah

Letter to my Daughters III

September 14th, 1996

m y dear daughters, I had secretly hoped I might be with you by today so that we could together break the fast of Ramazan. But because I could not yet join you, I imagined you instead. I pictured you three, your mother, and I gathered around the dastarkhan at Iftar and you girls bringing in the platters of naan and torshi, palao, chalow, and korma. I smelled the food and felt your hands touch mine as you passed me platter after platter. At that moment, lost in the image I'd created, I believed we were together. And when, after a few moments, I realized we were not, I would have relinquished all my accomplishments, handed them over to Allah with open palms, only to turn that image real.

The boy Amin feels my sorrow; after all these months meeting my simple needs, he has become attuned to me. At sunset, he entered quietly, bringing me first a dish of several dried dates. Then he brought in more food—not as much as I have imagined above, but plenty for me. He did not seem to want to go home, so I invited him to join me, and we sat together quietly, companionably.

He never looks directly at the pictures of you I keep tacked up in a corner of the room; he does not want to show disrespect. But I also imagine, as he is *human, that he has looked at them when I have been out of the room. On this occasion, he nodded his head toward them. "You have spoken with your family this week?" Of course he knows I have, since my phone calls are not secret, but he and the others do me the courtesy of pretending I have privacy, as if I had freedom.*

I nodded.

He stayed quiet, but I could sense him wrestling with a thought.

"Speak," I said after a minute.

He moved close and lowered his voice. "Doctor President," he began. This is usually what he calls me, as if searching for the proper title. "What if it were possible to arrange for you to leave here?"

"That's what I've been requesting of the UN all along, boy," I said, speaking gently, as I knew his intentions were good. "There have been many letters sent directly to the secretary-general."

"But Doctor President, I am not speaking of official avenues; they have proven useless. I am speaking of accessing a side door and going directly to the airport."

"Escape. That's what you imagine?"

He startled, surprised by my laughter, then nodded.

I thought of dismissing him, turning my back, eating alone. But I knew his heart was good, though he had much to learn.

"Let's consider it together," I said. "First, in practical terms. If I managed to get past the guards and slip out a side door, I would quickly be spotted on the street."

"We will have a disguise."

"That will hide my physique?"

"We will put you immediately in a car. It will be night."

"Ah. And rush me to the airport. And then what? A UN plane is out of

the question; they want their relationship with the donkey Rabbani to remain intact. A private plane cannot simply take off without an okay from the tower, and that is controlled by Rabbani loyalists. He's been smart there."

"This has been handled, Doctor President," the boy said. "We have those who support you with full hearts. Some always have; others have reconsidered their alliances. They include pilots willing to lie about the cargo they carry."

"You've thought it out, then, boy, have you?" I was impressed by young Amin and hesitated a moment, sorry to have to disappoint him. "But we must look at it from all angles. Is it not enough that my country has abandoned me? It's your plan that I will lower my head and dash from my home sheepishly, like a criminal or a defeated dog? This is the way you think I should secure my distance from the darkness?"

"Doctor President." He hesitated, then straightened his shoulders and went on boldly, "What are you worth to your country from here?"

"Amin. Do you remember last year when the UN's special envoy to Afghanistan suggested I use my kidney stones to get me out of the country? His thought was that I should claim to be more ill than I was. He imagined I would agree to be transported to the airport on a stretcher via ambulance in order to gain my freedom. I refused to take part in this ruse and leave in this manner. Even were I dying, I would not retreat like this, as if I had done something wrong."

"Doctor President, that was a year ago. Perhaps—forgive me, but perhaps then there was still time for such pride. I walk the streets that are forbidden to you. I hear the talk. The situation has worsened."

"Of course it has. The world will not find rest simply by saying the word 'peace.' It needs wise leaders, and those are lacking now."

"And so?"

"I will never agree to discard my own dignity," I said. "A man is as vast

as he acts, Amin. You are smart. You have developed a scheme for my departure, and you have thought to approach me on a night when I am weak, missing my family. The only matter you failed to foresee is that it is exactly for my family that I will not agree to leave like this. I will not pass on to my daughters the legacy of a coward."

He looked so sad, so defeated. He is a young man, and he thought he had a strategy for saving the great Najib. Who knows to how many he had spoken? What promises, however halfhearted, he had worked to extract?

"My son," I said, "why should we rush to buy twenty-five uncaught sparrows when all we really need is one in our hands? I will be out of here soon without these elaborate machinations made of air. I'm Muslim, and I am Pashtun. The fundamentalists are also Muslims and Pashtuns. They will not hurt me; they will banish me. I will be with my family soon enough. And together we will wait to return, because water will flow through this parched riverbed again."

And so, my daughters, through relaying this conversation with Amin, I say the same to you. Your father will not come home cowed. But he will come home. We will be together soon. And until then, you and your mother are with me in every dream I have.

I pass this sealed letter on to Amin to mail, its envelope filled with my love,

Najib

More Letters

Stela

September 14th

Dear General McChrystal,

This is another letter from Stela Sidorova. I am writing once again because I would still like to go over, in more detail, the criteria for awarding medals to fallen soldiers. My youngest son, Piotr, with surprising reddish hair, wanted to be a botanist—not unexpected given his lifelong refusal to kill the spiders we found in our house (he would capture them in a jar, keep them as pets a day or two, and then dump them outside). Anyway, I'm sure you can't remember the names of all the mothers who must correspond with you, nor of everyone who was awarded a Silver Medal, but my Piotr was one of those, and you can probably look him up somewhere, no?

Piotr Sidorov.

However, there have been questions about the circumstances of his death. I don't want to believe the officers of any army under your charge, as Piotr and his fellow soldiers were at that time, would ever be anything but honest with me. But I am wondering if you could reply and specify for me quite simply the circumstances of the award he was given posthumously. (Such a horrible word, isn't it? I imagine you dislike it as much as I do.) This would do much to set a mother's heart . . .

Dear Steve Coll,

Congratulations on your Pulitzer Prize. I am sorry to say I do not have your book in my shop, Bulgakov's Bookshelf. I would like to say it is because no one who ever buys that book wants to later sell it to a used bookstore. And I'm sure that is true, by the way. But I must be honest. In my case, the people who frequent my shop have very little interest in reading about Afghanistan. They live in a dream world, most of them, cut off from the pressing matters of our day.

I, however, checked your book out of the library and read it with great interest. I am writing to see if it is possible that, in your research, you came upon information about the Pech Valley and specific activities there. I am wondering if there are army records that give more details about fatalities than are given to family members of fallen soldiers. I have already written four polite letters to Gen. McChrystal and so far have received no reply. Should you have any details on this, I'd be so grateful if . . .

Dear Mr. Bob Dylan,

I believe you are the Pushkin of America. He was also very young when he began to be recognized, and he was a radical spokesman. A woman, of course, was his downfall, and you have managed to avoid that so far; I congratulate you. I read an old *Playboy* interview with you once—I don't subscribe, of course, but I received old issues from an estate sale for my bookstore, Bulgakov's Bookshelf—and in it, you were so sarcastic that I almost stopped reading, but I kept on, and I'm glad I did because you said something I still remember: "Art, if there is such a thing, is in the bathrooms; everybody knows that." Even if you meant that to also be sarcastic, I think my son Danil would agree.

I guess I'm late in telling you my name is Stela Sidorova, and I started reading about you because you were one of my other son's favorite musicians. Which always struck me as funny because Piotr was not of your generation. And also because he ended up enlisting to fight, and you were against war. So how much to heart could he have taken your lyrics? Forgive me for asking.

But now I wonder if maybe Piotr liked you because you wouldn't let people call you a prophet. It's an important question for me because they are calling my son a hero, and I wonder if maybe he wouldn't want that either. Do you believe labels are used deliberately to give life to lies? But how did your mother feel about the names they called you, good and bad? And I must ask you as a true skeptic: Don't we have to trust in something, at least a few of the big things, in order to . . .

Dear Danil, my beloved son,

You always protected him, and you are protecting him still, first from the bullies and now from the myth-makers and deceivers. I see that, and I know he would want it. But try to imagine what it is to be a mother. It's not an easy matter to accept losing a baby to a mistake. "Mistake" becomes a swear word, one that I could begin to pronounce only after I read the generals were withdrawing our troops from that place. The place where Piotr died. Leaving? Did it mean we'd won on that sour, unwelcome patch of ground? No, they said, it meant in fact that we couldn't win there, but they went on to say that was fine because we didn't need to win there. We didn't need to hold that territory. I wanted to scream: Why, then, was Piotr ever sent there?

And if that was a mistake, what else? Now I say it, though it breaks my heart: I fear what you told me may be true.

It's not that I doubted you, Danil. I know that's what you thought. It's that I couldn't face something that big and ugly lingering over the loss of Piotr. And yes, I didn't want you to sweep our dirt outside our house. I see now it wasn't *our* dirt.

I give you my blessings to speak your own honesty; you no longer have to keep your views secret in the world, if you wish. But please, Danil, rejoin me. Even if you are still angry, a bad peace is better than a good quarrel. I have sent you many letters; I've begun and thrown away even more. Please, please let me know you have received this, and that you are willing . . .

The Gallery

Danil

September 15th

1 'm so glad you sent me the photos, Danil," said Marco, the gallery owner. "Your work is strong. It fits thematically with what we're after. So here's what's happening. Some patrons with fat wallets and media connections want to bring attention to the war."

"Why?" Danil asked. "It's hardly a good-news story at this point. It seems to me most people are busy looking away."

Marco shrugged. He had the darkest eyes Danil had ever seen and an intimate way of speaking that made it seem as if he were sharing a secret. "Political reasons, personal reasons, moral reasons, who knows?" he said. "All I can tell you for sure is there's a strong commitment. They want this show ready in time for the anniversary of the invasion, for PR reasons, so they're pulling it together fast. Here's the vision."

Marco took Danil's arm and walked him away from the entrance into a second room with two brick walls and two white ones. "They'll put up large photos of your street pieces over here," he said, "so they'll be seen in the context of their locations. They have some other artists lined up, too. Plus work by some of the photojournalists who've been covering this. The pieces will sell; you'll get your cut. But here's the kicker, what makes this visionary, what will attract the media attention. On opening night, all these folks will come, wine, hors d'oeuvres, the usual. And they'll watch you." He gestured to one of the brick walls. "Right in front of them, you'll put a stenciled piece directly on the gallery wall. You'll have to show us what you're going to do in advance, of course, but the only thing we ask it that it be a new piece, and about war, like your others. Bring your spray cans, whatever you need. We'll put up a little caution-tape barricade, but people will be able to get close. We'll lower the lights a bit." He squeezed Danil's shoulder. "It'll be great. It's visual art, a political statement on several levels, but also performance art, and that makes it exciting. Of course the piece will have to be removed later, maybe in three weeks, to make way for the next show. But street art is transient anyway, right? And by then, it—and you, at work—will have already been photographed, videoed, interviewed."

"Videoed?" Danil wondered if that was even a word.

"So it'll give a bit of permanence to it, don't you think? And then, you're launched."

"My identity will be known?"

"If this is an issue, let's talk about it." Marco motioned Danil toward his office in a corner of the gallery behind a glass wall. "We don't want you to get stuck doing community service," he laughed, "and a mask might be interesting. But if you let them see your face, it fits with what this is all about. We want to call the show Transparent War."

"'Transparent'?"

"As in laid bare, through your work and the others'." Marco sat at his desk. "Truth, they say, is the first casualty, right? The backers of this show want to get at that." He tapped a thermos in his office. "Coffee?" Danil nodded, and Marco poured him a cup. "Black okay? Anyway, it's going to be a good show, on several levels. Plus, I believe you'll end up making some real money in time. People will hire you to put up stencils in various locations. You'll do some speaking, if you want. Maybe the college circuit for a year. Professors will know that you'll connect with their students."

Marco struck Danil as passionate but only halfway genuine, a salesman first of all. And he himself was being handled like a potential big buyer. "Sounds a bit unlikely to me," he said.

"That's what we want. We don't want to do the usual."

"And also . . ."

"'Commercial' is what you're going to say," Marco interrupted. "Look, I know, my friend, I get it. This is a private commemoration of your brother. A war hero; I heard about him. Silver Medal. Goddamn, I'm sorry. But look at it this way. This will just broaden the respect he's given."

"I don't want my . . . I don't want him part of it."

A slight expression of annoyance swept across Marco's face, but only for a second. "I understand. But I mean, people are going to ask about your connection to the work and all, and your brother, well, it's a natural . . . it might creep into the publicity material even if we try to keep it out. But, Danil, this is an amazing thing to fall in your lap. I know you've got your questions, but—forgive me for being frank here—I did expect some more enthusiasm."

Danil stepped out of the office and over to one of the brick walls. He ran his hand along it, feeling the texture, the mortar between the bricks, glad for something solid. He could picture a piece on the space. But what about the promise he'd made his mother to keep the real story to himself? Didn't she have a claim to Piotr's memory, too? "I need a couple days," he said to Marco, who'd followed him.

"I know there's no money up front—" Marco began.

"It's not that."

Marco looked at him directly for the first time, as if sizing him up. "Okay. But do get back to me by Thursday afternoon, no later. If I don't hear from you, I'm going to figure this is a no. I mean, one of our benefactors specifically chose your work, Danil. But we do face some time constraints here, so if I have to find someone else . . ."

"Yeah, thanks. I just have to think it through a little more. I appreciate your understanding."

On the way to the subway, he texted Joni: "Met the gallery owner. He's got big plans."

Before he went underground, he got her reply: "Don't turn your back on this, Danil. This could be your break. You hear me?"

His break. Sure, but. Though he hadn't been able to tell Joni everything, he'd mentioned unidentified, pressing family issues. She'd been clear about her viewpoint. "Do what you have to do for the work, and your future," she'd said. "Don't ignore an opportunity. Take no prisoners."

It wasn't so simple.

What if his "break" collided with his commitments? This work was supposed to be his private, principled response to an immoral situation. How could he justify letting it end up breaking a heart already shattered once before?

Maiwand Hospital

Mandy

September 15th

first she had to sidestep through a slender entrance to Maiwand Hospital, past an armed guard and beneath a large sign of a gun with a red line through it indicating she was not to carry weapons. As if someone doubted her word about that, a woman right inside the entrance patted her down. Then she stood to one side of the courtyard watching others negotiate their way into the hospital until another woman arrived, introduced herself as Zarlasht, and said she would accompany Mandy on her tour. She was not warm and did not seem thrilled to have Mandy visiting or to even understand why she was there. Her English, however, was clearly excellent.

Mandy handed over a large box of supplies, which Zarlasht gave to a young man dressed in white, an orderly. "Thank you. It will be distributed," she said.

"I'm a nurse and nurse trainer," Mandy said. "Specifically emergency room—I don't know if they told you. Maybe I could meet . . ."

But Zarlasht was already walking ahead. "We'll stop there first," she said over her shoulder.

The long, narrow emergency hall, to the left of the entrance, was teeming with people, so choked that Mandy saw they couldn't enter without pushing others aside. It was dark, and dense with the scent of blood. Mandy looked at Zarlasht, whose face gave nothing away, and then she plunged forward. This was why she was here, wasn't it?

Managing to steer through the clogged entryway, she reached a hallway that opened up slightly into a wider room, still overcrowded. Some people supported wounded patients; others slumped on the floor or leaned limply against a wall. A few lay on stretchers. Mandy wondered what had happened; some had visible signs of trauma such as bleeding from a limb, but most did not. One hospital employee seemed to be taking down information from those in a line. At first she didn't see any medical personnel; then she picked out two doctors and one nurse. They were clearly overwhelmed by whatever disaster had occurred; they didn't even notice her. She wanted to spend time here but understood that right now her presence would simply add to the chaos.

She pushed her way back out to where Zarlasht waited. "What happened?" Mandy asked.

"What do you mean?'

"An attack? An accident?"

Zarlasht looked at her with a combination of doubt and derision. "This is always how it is."

Mandy tried to recover quickly. "Maybe we could set up a time for me to meet with the nurses, talk about how they work?" she suggested.

"Maybe," Zarlasht said in a way that seemed to Mandy to mean no. "For now, I suggest the children's wing."

"Sure," Mandy agreed. She had to be flexible and try to learn something if she couldn't teach something. Zarlasht led her through a large garden. Perhaps a dozen families had set up impromptu camps with food supplies, blankets, and an occasional suitcase. "These are visitors?" Mandy asked.

"If they live far away and don't have family in Kabul, they stay the nights here," Zarlasht said. "We don't have accommodations for them anywhere else."

Mandy had the sense that every question she asked seemed stupid. She vowed to be silent for a while.

The building that housed the pediatrics ward had surely never been attractive. Now it stood in decay, crumbling in places, and worse, with no sense that anything had been sterilized or even fully cleaned. Still, it felt spacious and calm in comparison to the emergency room.

On the ground floor, they went from room to room visiting children lying on beds, covered with blankets made of gauze-like material, most with a family member or two at their side. Many children appeared to sleep, though a couple of boys sat up when they entered, and one toddler, a girl wearing blue pants, no shirt, and a colorful necklace, smiled slightly at them. The relatives—usually mothers or grandmothers, Mandy guessed—sat quietly on the edges of beds, often appearing exhausted, uninterested. She saw no IVs or monitoring equipment.

They took the stairs to the second floor, which felt more crowded, and again they went from room to room. Again Mandy saw virtually no equipment; the wing felt more like it belonged to a drab and underfurnished college dormitory than to a hospital.

"You can see, of course, that we need more nurses," Zarlasht said, her tone proprietary, as if offering Mandy a job. "The ones we have don't last. The job is stressful; the pay is low; and with large parts of the country in disarray, many have troubles at home."

"And besides staffing? What do you need most in terms of supplies?"

"The list is long. We need a new emergency room and more up-to-date monitoring equipment. We need a modern operating room." Zarlasht shook her head. "We're a teaching hospital. I sometimes wonder what lessons the young doctors learn here."

Mandy felt a rush of shame. What could she do here? How could she have done so little preparation to assess needs? "My antibiotics and sterile bandages don't do much," she said apologetically.

"We're happy to have them."

"I can reach out to my own hospital when I'm home," Mandy said. "Try to get more to send you."

Zarlasht nodded. "I will make sure you know how to reach me."

Now, in each room, Mandy sought to linger longer. She wished she'd thought to bring something for each child. "Can you buy balloons in Kabul?" she asked Zarlasht as they moved up to the third floor. Zarlasht repeated the word with a puzzled look.

The top floor was crowded. Its rooms held children who had lost limbs. There were no elevators, so patients had to be wheeled up ramps, and Mandy wondered—but did not ask—about the decision to house them on the top floor. In one corner, an open closet revealed several pairs of small crutches. Zarlasht, seeing this, raised her voice, speaking sternly to a nurse who responded by reaching into a front pocket of her dress, pulling out a key, and hurrying to close and lock the closet. "An Italian charity sends us the crutches,"

Zarlasht explained. "But if the closet is left unlocked, the visitors steal them to give to others. Then we don't have enough for our own patients."

Mandy hesitated outside the door of a room. "What about physical therapy?"

"We don't have that here. A center in Kabul is very active in this field, but it treats only men."

They entered the room together. A girl, about thirteen, sat up in her bed. She'd lost both legs directly above the knees; this was clear by the way the sheet lay. She was alone, with a calm but half-dazed look on her face. Mandy suddenly felt frozen by a sense of futility. She was physically unable to enter the room. Before, she'd always believed her work as a nurse contributed to the world, at least enough. If she'd considered it, she would have said grown-ups were too busy being productive to focus on elusive concepts that might have consumed them in adolescence, like life's meaning. Since Jimmy, though, she'd been fighting against a feeling of hopelessness nipping at the edges of her being. She'd found herself thinking that any single human act is ultimately useless; then she would argue with herself about this, though never decisively. Now, looking at the girl, an unlikely mirror of her own son, she felt she'd irretrievably lost the argument. And she felt angry with herself. Having good intentions wasn't enough.

Tears pressed against the backs of her eyes. She pulled a water bottle out of her bag and took a sip. Zarlasht, she saw, was speaking to the nurse she'd earlier scolded. Mandy slipped out into the hallway, needing a few moments of relative aloneness. But the hallway offered no benches or even folding chairs, so she sat on the steps. Something sticky had spilled on one of them, she saw, and dust clung to the corners. She hadn't expected to feel so overwhelmed; this was not the time for self-pity or esoteric internal arguments. She needed to gather herself, and she would try to do it quickly.

She was alone for only a moment, though, before she felt someone beside her. Zarlasht.

"For a nurse, you are—what is the word? Not so able to look at medical things," Zarlasht said. Though Mandy knew she probably deserved derision, Zarlasht's voice was not unkind.

She gave an apologetic half laugh. "Squeamish."

"'Squeamish,'" Zarlasht repeated.

"Not normally. Today . . ." Mandy trailed off.

"The steps are not so good for sitting," Zarlasht said. "Come with me."

Mandy really wanted a few minutes alone, but privacy no longer seemed an option. She followed Zarlasht down the hall and into a small room with a desk and three chairs. A moment later, the same nurse Zarlasht had earlier scolded arrived with two cups of hot *chai* and a plate of a half-dozen candies wrapped in colorful foil.

"Thank you," Mandy said, "that's so kind. I'm sorry. I'm all right. It's only that . . ."

"Drink *chai* first," Zarlasht said. "Then we can talk."

Gratefully, Mandy sipped the *chai*. Zarlasht seemed comfortable with the silence, which Mandy appreciated. "My son," she began after a few minutes, "came to Afghanistan as a soldier several years ago. He lost both his legs here. Roadside bomb."

Zarlasht nodded. "I'm sorry for you and your son," she said, her voice kind but matter-of-fact. "This girl? The one you just saw? We will be able to get her prosthetics, *inshallah*. If the aid does not dry up. But she will never marry. She will not go to school. Her family will feel shamed by her. She will not have ongoing medical care." She shook her head. "Real recovery for her is not possible."

Mandy nodded. "In that context, my son was lucky."

Zarlasht studied Mandy for a moment, then shook her head. "It is poor luck on all sides."

"Do you have children, Zarlasht?"

"A daughter. Two sons."

"Then you know what it is . . ."

"To see one of them hurt? Yes, I know." She hesitated, then added, "Compassion is a luxury here. We don't have extra to spare."

Mandy suddenly felt the settling in of a deep-seated weariness. "Thank you for sharing the girl's story," she said.

"I think it is enough for this time," Zarlasht said, touching above her heart with her right hand.

Mandy did not protest. She was glad that she'd have the rest of the afternoon to herself. Her visit to the refugee camp was not until tomorrow.

"If you still want, I will try to set up a session with some of the nurses."

"That would be wonderful," Mandy said.

Zarlasht leaned forward. "It is hard," she said softly, "to be a woman in this country."

"I'm learning that."

"And when you are a strong woman, men don't like it."

"Maybe it will change, in time." Mandy knew this was not a meaningful response, but the conversation was taking a turn she didn't quite understand. She felt something else was expected of her, but she didn't know what.

"You have connection with Amin, yes?" Zarlasht asked.

"We met with him at the beginning, after Todd, Mr. Barbery—" Mandy hesitated, as though it were somehow impolite to mention the kidnapping.

"And you can speak with Amin now?"

Mandy shook her head. "He's traveling. A driver from his office brought me here."

"But you can pass on a message to the driver? Ask him to get it to Amin urgently?"

"Yes," Mandy said, surprised. "I can try."

"He will do it if you insist. You are a foreign woman. Amin must be told to remember that if Najib had agreed to leave, the story would have ended differently."

Najib? Story? Mandy wasn't sure what Zarlasht meant, but on its surface, the message hardly seemed urgent. Still, she felt Zarlasht's intensity.

"Can you write it down, to make sure you remember these exact words?" Zarlasht got up and produced a pen and paper from the desk. Mandy bent over to write. Zarlasht read over her shoulder, and then nodded. "He should be given this message right away," she said. "Today. As soon as you leave here. You can do that?"

"Sure. I'll ask the driver."

"Make certain Amin is told."

Mandy looked directly at Zarlasht. "Can you tell me what it means?"

Zarlasht hesitated a moment. "It means I believe in friendship between our countries, too," she said. "Or at least between individuals from our two countries." Then she gestured, leading Mandy back down the stairs, past the emergency room, back to the entrance. She bade Mandy good-bye with two final words—"Make certain"—and watched as Mandy headed out of Maiwand and onto the Kabul street where her driver waited.

A Call in the Dark

Clarissa

September 16th

C larissa reached her hand through the dark, lifting the noisy receiver and pressing it to her ear. "Hello," she said, not fully awake but already beginning to feel adrenaline run through her.

"This is the wife of Todd Barbery?"

The kidnappers. She knew it. She couldn't speak.

"Hello?"

"Yes," she managed.

"Wife of Todd Barbery?"

"Yes," she said. "This is Todd's wife."

"Good. I want you to hear from our guest."

"Who is this?" she asked. She heard the sound of a muffled voice, something said in the background that she couldn't make out.

"Hello?" It was Todd's voice.

"Oh, my God."

"Clari."

"Todd. I love you."

"I love you, too."

"Are you okay?" She was standing now, grabbing a pen to take notes, even though they were surely recording the call.

"Yes. I'm fine. I miss you, but I'm fine. Worrying about you."

"We're all good here, Todd. Ruby's fine, too. We're strong. We're fine. We're working to get you home, that's all."

"Clari, I'm sorry." His voice faltered. "Really sorry."

"Todd, it's not your fault." Clarissa took a deep breath so that her own voice would sound solid, would give him strength. She tried to think: What had Jack told her? What was she supposed to say? "Is there anything you want me to know, Todd?"

"I'm all right. They said I could tell you that at least."

"Any advice for us? Anything we should be doing?"

"Just keep—" Todd broke off. Clarissa heard a rustle, the sound of the phone changing hands.

"So you see, wife of Todd Barbery, that your husband is fine."

"Wait! I'm not—"

"Listen to me. He is fine for now. Your negotiators need to respond to our requests. Time is important. You understand?"

"Yes, but—"

"We are not interested in a conversation with you. Only pass this information. You understand?"

"Yes, but—"

"Good-bye, then, Todd Barbery's wife."

And the line went fully, frustratingly dead.

Kitchen Conversations

Danil

September 17th

danil hung in a breath of space, frozen, as if he were one of the pinned butterflies Piotr used to collect. He lifted his hand, hesitated, then rang the doorbell, committing himself. Within a heartbeat, he regretted it. He half-turned away, imagined dashing down the street, ducking behind a car, and realized how bizarre that behavior would be. He turned back just as the door opened. A woman about his age stood there in jeans and boots, her hair pulled back.

"Yes?" She looked stern and puzzled.

"I'm here to see Clarissa."

"Are you with the . . . ?" She trailed off, obviously taking in his paint-stained shirt and jeans stretched at the seams. "Who are you?"

"No one, I'm just . . ." He suddenly put it together. "You must be Ruby."

She took a half step back, distrust on her face.

"Clarissa gave me some food you'd made."

Her eyes narrowed.

"It was delicious."

She neither replied nor moved.

"Is Clarissa here?"

"What's this about?" she said.

"Ruby?" He heard Clarissa's voice and then could see her coming down the stairs, behind Ruby, rubbing her damp hair with a towel. She seemed distracted but oddly unsurprised to see him. "Hi," she said to both Ruby and Danil at once.

"The door was unlocked, so I—" Ruby began

"Sure, of course," Clarissa said. "You two have introduced your-selves?"

Danil glanced at Ruby. "Actually, I'm not sure I . . ."

"This is Danil," Clarissa said. "He's an artist. And this is Ruby. Todd's daughter. Come in." She gestured toward Danil.

"Thanks," he said, but even before he could step in, two men pushed open the gate from the street and walked up behind him.

"This is my brother, Mikey," Clarissa said, speaking quickly now. "And Todd's boss, Bill. Mikey and Bill, meet Danil."

"Does he know my dad?" Ruby said.

Clarissa shook her head.

"Is this a bad time?" Danil asked. Clearly it was, but he'd had to work up to this moment once and didn't know if he could do it again.

"Come in, all of you," Clarissa repeated, adding directly to Danil, "you, too."

Danil stepped in, shaking hands with the two men. They moved as a group toward the kitchen. Danil hung back.

"Not a social call, is it?" Clarissa asked, hesitating outside the kitchen door.

Danil leaned toward her. "I wanted to . . . ask you about some-thing . . . but I'm sorry, this isn't . . ."

"No, it's fine. You guys help yourself to juice or whatever," she said to the others, and then turned to him. "I heard from Todd. The FBI wants to give us some guidance based on that. But we have a few minutes."

"Oh, man," Danil said. "I can't interrupt—"

"Let's go in here," Clarissa said.

She sat on the bench in the entryway, and he joined her. He knew she didn't have much time, so he started right in. "It's about my brother, and . . ." He knew he sounded inarticulate. "I feel kind of silly."

"It's okay. Go on."

"There's this gallery owner in the city, and he's offered me a place in a show."

"Danil. That's great."

"But there's an issue to do with my mom and my brother and what happened in Afghanistan. I haven't talked to anyone . . . and I thought maybe you . . ." Clarissa leaned toward him, listening in a concentrated way.

"Clarissa." It was the daughter. "Any minute now."

"I'll be right there," Clarissa said without looking away from Danil.

The phone rang, and Danil saw Ruby move to pick it up. She set the receiver in the middle of the table.

"I'm sorry. This is rude."

"Danil, listen," Clarissa said in a hushed tone. "I've already talked to the FBI once today; this is really more for everyone else. It should take under fifteen minutes. Then I'd like to hear your question. Really I would. So please just stay."

"Clarissa," Ruby, who'd approached them, said in a loud voice, "Jack told us not to—"

"Danil already knows, Ruby."

Ruby raised her eyebrows, and her lips, impossibly, narrowed.

"He lost a brother in Afghanistan," Clarissa said, as though that would explain everything to the daughter.

"I'll go," Danil said.

"Stay here." Clarissa's tone held authority. "Fifteen minutes. Ruby, is Jack on speaker?"

Until now, Danil had mainly seen uncertainty and vulnerability in Clarissa. But at this moment, everyone moved to follow her instructions, even Ruby. He could see Clarissa must be capable in her other life, the one she'd lived prior to what had happened to her husband. How far had she already traveled from that existence, he wondered, and how long would it take her to get back? It doesn't matter how distant you stay from the grenade launchers and helicopters, the carbine assault rifles and the battle tanks; war poisons the air half a world away and then travels on the wind to slip into your peaceful lungs, changing everything.

He knew that he should leave, but, like the others, Danil followed Clarissa's orders. He lounged on the cushioned bench, feeling tired now, worn out by his night work and the energy it had taken to come to this house and initiate this conversation.

Though he was in another room, he could see the four of them sitting around the kitchen table and hear the disembodied male voice coming from the speakerphone. It seemed the authorities had nothing new to report about Clarissa's husband. "It's not like a television show; things don't always happen between commercials," the voice said. The man sounded calm and friendly. But Danil felt a rush of distrust, knowing that a level of bureaucracy, combined with covert political concerns and a wide river of details that fell under the umbrella of "national security," all tended to disguise facts and smudge meanings. He wondered how much of that Clarissa had already discovered.

The group talked for about ten minutes, and the mumble of their voices turned into Piotr's voice. "It's weird," Piotr had told him in one of their few overseas phone conversations. "In some ways, I feel faceless here, the proverbial cog in the wheel. In others, Dani, I feel like I belong. For the first time in my life."

"You didn't feel that before?" Danil knew he sounded a little hurt.

"You know what I mean. We need each other here."

"*I* need you, bro." Danil startled even as he said it. He'd been so clear about Piotr needing *him* that he hadn't realized until that moment that it went the other way, too.

"I know, man," Piotr had said, struggling for the words. "But everything's different over here. All we've got is each other. You get all these dark thoughts—" He broke off, giving up. "Anyway, this is only for now. I'll be home soon."

The voice of Clarissa's stepdaughter, tight with tension, interrupted Danil's thoughts. "I don't know what we're waiting for. Do we trust the word of some Afghan kidnappers more than we trust our own troops?"

"I agree, Ruby," said the voice on the phone.

There was a moment of silence before Clarissa spoke. "I know it's frustrating," she said. "But Amin is in negotiations right now. I want to stick it out. If something changes on the ground, Jack, you will let us know."

A few minutes later, they hung up. The daughter rose, noisily got herself a glass of water, and sank back down. "I still don't agree," she said, her voice strained.

Danil realized they'd forgotten he was there. He wondered if he should clear his throat to remind them, but before he could decide, the husband's boss spoke up. "I know it's hard, Ruby," he said, "but I strongly advocate leaving this in Amin's hands a little longer."

"It's more than hard, Bill."

"Look, I'll say it again," the boss said. "As soon as you introduce guns, any situation has the potential to become more chaotic. Mix in cultural and language divides, and it's combustible. Besides, the Americans are juggling a lot of balls. One kidnapped relief worker is only part of the picture for them. Amin's interests are not muddied."

"How can he succeed without money for ransom?" the daughter asked.

"There are long-standing relationships between families that are beyond our understanding."

"When do you speak to Amin next?" the daughter asked.

"Later today, I expect," the boss answered. "Tomorrow at the latest."

"Well," the daughter said after a moment of silence, her voice dense with frustration, "I have to go."

"Ruby," Clarissa's brother said. "We're all trying to do the right thing here."

"I just wish we agreed on what that was."

By now, Danil had shrunk back into the corner of the room and was deeply regretting not slipping away half an hour earlier. Ruby shot past the sitting room and through the front door without glancing in his direction. He heard the boss murmur something to Clarissa in a soothing tone and follow the daughter out.

"Clari, hang in there," her brother said. "I'll call you tonight, okay?"

After the brother left, Danil peeked into the kitchen and saw Clarissa sitting with her forehead resting in the palm of her hand. He backed up and bumped into a chair.

"Danil." Clarissa rose and came into the room. "I'm sorry. I got so caught up that I forgot—"

"I should have left."

"I think you were trying to. I wouldn't let you." Clarissa smiled wryly.

"I'm going to get out of your hair."

"Not yet. Talking to you is actually helpful for me."

"So what did he say, your husband?"

"Not much. Maybe twenty words. He sounded okay. But it was too fast. I'm trying to process everything. All I'm managing to do is be present for the FBI briefings; the rest of my life is complete confusion. And even during the briefings, I can't seem to handle it right."

"I don't know if there is a right way."

"No, there is, there must be. Todd's daughter, she's . . . she's angry with me. She thinks I'm crazy—or maybe something worse than crazy. She can't understand why I can't just trust them. I almost want to give in for her sake; we don't need tension between us right now, and Todd wouldn't want it." Then she turned to him. "What you went through was harder, Danil; of course I know that."

Danil raised his head to meet her gaze. "My brother," he said, "was killed by friendly fire."

She put her hand to her mouth and then lowered it again. She sat. Danil remained standing. The words came slowly. He hadn't spoken to anyone about this in so long.

"They didn't tell us at first," he said. "They claimed he was killed by enemy mortar during a firefight." He felt a surge of anger and wondered when—if—it would diminish. He hesitated for a beat, but now that he'd begun, he felt like a plug had been yanked from the drain. "They expanded the story, even. They said he was trying to drag a wounded soldier to safety when he was killed. They said he was being awarded a distinguished service medal, that it had already been approved. My mom got a letter from the president." He made a scoffing sound. "But something never felt right to me. I tried to explain it to my mother, but it sounded like I was one of those people who thinks 9/11 was a U.S. conspiracy. She thinks she can read people, and she was convinced they were telling her the truth. Then one day, out of the blue, a soldier in my brother's unit called me. He told me it didn't actually go down the way the army said. I wasn't surprised. But to hear it said baldly like that—I was kind of. . . ." He paused, pulled in his breath. "I wanted the details. The reason I went to Afghanistan? To look my brother's commander in the eye. To tell him my brother thought these guys were his best friends. And it worked. Person to person, he came clean. He told me he never wanted to keep it secret in the first place."

"How'd it happen?"

"They'd been airlifted to this area in the middle of fucking no-where in the dead of night. They were told to wait until dawn, and then they began foot-patrolling the outskirts of some village that they thought held al-Qaeda or Taliban. Insurgents, terrorists—what the hell, probably just a bunch of farmers with guns. They spent a couple hours climbing down steep mountainsides, searching cran-nies in between rocks for stored weapons or ammunition. Finally they were on their way out when they got pinned down by small-arms fire that seemed to come from across a ridge. It was morning, about 10:20. They ducked and radioed in coordinates. There was some kind of malfunction with the tactical communication sys-tems, but one second lieutenant was able to radio information out. The military sent in airpower as backup. Either the pilot got con-fused or the right message never reached him. It was chaotic, and I think that's how it is more often than we know. These guys were in firefights about every other day. They'd lost four soldiers over the previous month. They were probably all mentally fried. My brother was killed by cannon fire from a low-flying F-18 on a straf-ing run."

"Oh, God."

Danil's legs suddenly felt heavy; he sat down. "But there were all kinds of PR reasons not to record it that way. When I got back, I tried to contact our liaison—they give you a liaison when you lose a relative at war. I left a message—a mistake—and told him what I knew and pushed for an investigation. He didn't call me back for weeks. When I got ahold of him finally, he said they'd done an inter-nal investigation, and the friendly-fire allegation wasn't true."

"What?"

"Yeah. Can you believe it? So then I tried to contact my brother's commander again, and I never have been able to reach him. It goes on from there; I spent a lot of time trying to be heard. Trying to get an inquest. They kept sending me reports that showed he was killed by enemy fire. During that period, I did my first street art about the war. And it felt more satisfying than all the struggling, and more important for my brother, in some crazy way. So I stopped. I stopped all those efforts to correct the official records and I put my frustration into the work."

"Danil." She shook her head.

"But here's the deal. My mother won't accept it. She insists my brother was killed by al-Qaeda—not the Taliban, not farmers pissed off by the foreigners on their land, and certainly not fellow Americans. For her, that's the only way he's a hero, if a bunch of internationally recognized terrorists killed him. That's the only way she can accept that he's gone. I told her the two have nothing to do with one another, that Piotr is a hero, and he was before he went to war, but—" He broke off.

"That's hard."

"We aren't talking anymore," he said. "But before we stopped talking, she begged me not to tell anyone what happened. What I *say* happened; that's how she puts it. And I promised."

Clarissa drew in a breath.

"Yeah," Danil said. "So that's the problem with doing a show and getting asked questions about my brother. I'm not supposed to tell the real story."

Clarissa looked at her hands. "Can't you call your mother?" she said after a moment. "Tell her what's happening?"

"Every conversation we've had around this topic has gone pretty bad."

"That can't be what she wants, either."

Danil shook his head and gave a small laugh. "She's tough, my mom. She's a character."

"Tough or not," Clarissa said, "no one wants to lose twice." She took an audible breath. "I'm sure about that," she said.

Danil stared for a moment, letting her words sink in before he rose to go. She followed him to the door, and he turned to her, hovering for a moment. "Thank you," he said.

"Of course."

"You know, about the rescue attempt . . ."

"Yeah?" She studied him. "You got any advice?"

He shook his head. "I don't know what you should do; I wouldn't want your responsibility. But . . ." He hesitated, and she waited for him. "I wouldn't be too anxious to send in a rescue team. Like your husband's boss, I'd be worried about mistakes in the heat of battle, too."

Retaliation

Clarissa

September 18th

Clarissa glanced at the caller ID and then lifted the phone gingerly to her ear. "Hello?"

"Did you hear the news this morning?"

"I did, Ruby."

"Sixteen Afghans dead. Four of them children."

"I heard." In fact, she'd already talked to Bill, left a message on Jack's phone, and had time to be grateful that Ruby generally stayed up late and got up late.

"A wedding party, Clarissa. Could anti-American sentiment get any higher?"

Clarissa didn't respond.

"I'm afraid they'll retaliate against the man they've got in their hands."

"Oh, Ruby—"

"We've got to get him out."

"I agree."

"Good. So let's okay a rescue attempt. Today. Now."

"Ruby, we don't even know if a rescue attempt is possible right now. I'm still waiting to hear—"

"I'm not arguing this over the phone," Ruby said. "I'm coming over." And then the line went dead.

Compromise

Amin

September 18th

min, his uncle, one of the elders, and the elder's son had been sitting in silence for ten minutes—a silence that had grown suffocating and large. Amin wanted to apologize for somehow missing crucial clues, throwing the *jirga* process into disarray. There were local issues he didn't understand, dynamics he couldn't follow. But some things he knew: he knew it would be seen as arrogant of him to speak first, so he had to wait until they signaled they were ready. He knew his uncle's disappointment had grown deep; he knew the elder was here only out of friendship to his uncle but would feel no regret in turning his back on Amin if there were further missteps. He knew he somehow had to avoid those missteps if he was to have a chance of securing Mr. Todd's release.

These were men of his blood, but Samira had been right: he barely knew them. They didn't know him, either. They were strangers with a tangle of motivations and desires hidden behind lips that sometimes twitched with a craving to tell. They were men who shared an Afghan conviction that trust, like sunsets, looked different at the end of each day. He wished that he and the elder had time to speak without ceremony, without purpose, the way a dirt road can wander. Then, instead of using sterile words like "honor," they might have been able to discuss the unlikely ties between people, the urgency of human compassion, the promise of second chances.

The elder cleared his throat. "Tension has grown," he said at last. "Perhaps you've heard."

Amin nodded. "But that's not—"

"With the waves of anger so high," the elder interrupted Amin as his uncle shot him a look that ordered silence, "this situation could be taken out of our hands soon. It may even be too late now."

The elder's son got up and poured more *chai* for his father and then offered it to the others, who shook their heads.

"However," the elder began again after another moment, "if you will guarantee that once freed, this man will leave immediately and never return, never have further contact with our people of any sort, we might have a way to move forward. *Might.*"

Zarlasht had been right. The message she had sent had pointed to this compromise. It made her involvement clear, but the nature of that involvement remained fuzzy, slightly beyond the edge of his vision. Still, what felt important at the moment was her effort to help. Now it was up to him.

Amin put down his cup. "You mean this one, particular American?" he asked. "If this one American leaves and never returns, that would feel like justice?"

"Ah, justice," said the elder. "Justice is complicated with the Americans. But it is this one particular American you are interested in, isn't it? Or are there others?"

The elder's son dropped a smile into his open palm.

"Yes. In Allah's name, it is his release I seek," Amin said.

"In this case, I think it may be possible. If we have that assurance, *inshallah*, we will hope to move forward."

"We appreciate your enormous efforts on my nephew's behalf," his uncle told the elder, and then turned a pointed gaze toward Amin, opening his hands wide in question.

It seemed simple enough on the surface, almost too easy, a compromise Amin should gracefully and thankfully accept. But he'd already walked this path once, a million years ago at another point in his own history and the history of his country. He'd arranged everything based on his personal guarantee to everyone that a man would leave. He'd made complex preparations, confident the man would understand the urgency. And then that man's pride had been larger than his fear. Amin had been young, but he'd trusted his reading of a situation, and he'd been wrong. He'd failed. The echoes were eerie.

"Mr. Todd is my boss, not the other way around," Amin said.

"Yet this is your country," the elder said. "And your negotiation."

"That's right, Amin," said his uncle. "You must lead him in the required direction."

They were all looking at him. Now it had become his turn to speak. If he gave the complex, more honest answer, the elder would stand, bow politely, and leave, and his uncle would send Amin on his way. If he gave the "right" one, the elder would stand, bow politely, and leave, but then he would set something in motion. And that was why Amin had come here, after all.

But if Mr. Todd refused to depart, or felt insulted by a request that he promise never to return, this time Amin would not be spared, nor would his family. For making pledges he couldn't keep, Amin would be punished. He was being asked to vouch for the borders of another man's stubbornness or sense of duty. For the sake of Mr. Todd, he could promise anything. For the sake of his wife, uncle, and children, he couldn't make a promise that fell beyond his reach.

He felt three pairs of eyes upon him. He bowed his head and made a silent prayer to Allah for strength to make the right choice, say the right words. He lifted his cup and drained the last sip of *chai*. Then he opened his mouth, uncertain what would emerge until he began to speak, trusting in a wisdom greater than his for guidance.

Zer Sha, Zer Sha

Todd

September 19th

t odd groaned, forced awake by a jab in his still painful ribs. Not the end of a weapon, though—he knew what that felt like by now—so he registered it as not critically important and, seeing through squinted eyes that it was not yet dawn, turned away, unwilling to abandon sleep. It was almost morning of the fifteenth day since he'd been kidnapped, and sleep had become his escape. He knew he had to be careful, to guard against depression, keep his mind sharp, his body strong. But he also had to control anxiety and fears for the future. For the moment, maintaining that control seemed to require more time lost within dreams.

He felt another prod. "Get up."

He cracked his eyes to see a bare foot kicking his chest, a little harder this time. "Stop," he said. "No." Though he spoke without conviction, he felt proud of asserting himself.

"Get up!" He knew from the voice that it was the youngest guard, the one he'd privately nicknamed Fuzzy because of the quality of his beard. "You're moving."

Moving? Where?

Get up, Mr. Todd. Amin's voice, an instruction he had to obey. Todd groaned again, pushed himself to a sitting position, rubbed his eyes.

Moving? Why?

Calm, he told himself. *Be calm.* No point in getting alarmed over indecipherable implications. Moving meant there would soon be fresh air on his face, the outward swing of legs stifled too long, the joy in comparative freedom, even if it were brief, even if he were soon shoved into a car trunk, a cargo of hidden, fervent fear. Even if each move so far had brought him to a place worse than the one before, closer to the chaos of Pakistan's border, farther from the relative civility of Kabul.

He felt his heart and breathing speed up, becoming a song. Badabumpbumpbump badabumpbumpbump badabumpbumpbump. This was what it felt like to be truly alone, even among others: one formed a tight alliance with one's own breath and heartbeat, finding comfort in that internal language and no other. He shifted to his knees on the way to standing.

"*Zer sha, zer sha, zer sha.*" His guard, strident, raising his voice as if saying "move it" repeatedly could improve Todd's speed. Keep someone isolated and largely immobile for too many days, cut his leg, batter his ribs, and you cannot expect him to be able suddenly to run. This boy, however, would not care about this.

Now the barrel of a gun was shoved in his side. Steel encouragement from another guard. It was the tall, fidgety one who'd hurt Todd before. The dangerous one. He hadn't noticed that guard in the room; he'd been standing in the shadow of a corner.

Okay, then. "Okay, okay." *Don't think. Just move.*

He rose, pulling up the pants they'd given him, tying them tighter around his waist, which was narrowing. "Some *chai*?" he asked.

"No time," replied the taller one.

"Why must we move so quickly?"

No answer.

"Is there some news?"

Still no answer.

"Has anyone spoken to Clarissa?"

For this, he knew there would be no answer, but he wanted to say her name aloud now. A talisman, a lucky charm.

"*Zer sha, zer sha, zer sha,*" repeated Fuzzy.

"I'm *zer sha*-ing," Todd said under his breath.

Another shove from the gun. "Now."

"Do I take my blanket?" Todd lifted it as he spoke. For the last two moves, he'd been instructed to carry his bedding with him. He'd grown fond of it.

The taller fired his gun into the wall, and Todd jumped. "Leave it. And move," he said, pointing the gun at Todd.

So this was it. They were going to kill him. With this urgency, and this guard, and no pretense even of respect or continuity, what else could it be? Todd couldn't speak. Maybe he should try to escape right now, an effort that of course would fail, but then perhaps they would shoot him immediately instead of dragging this out. On the other hand, they might just beat him more. He glanced around the room, hesitating. Seeing the Bible, he tucked it under his arm without asking.

The taller guard kept his gun trained on Todd as he stepped through the doorway, into the main room, and then out into the yard, still trying to sift his choices through his mind. Right beyond the yard stood the car, motor running.

Todd turned to the guards. "Why?" he asked, repeating it. "Why?"

Of course no one answered. The tall one used his gun to motion Todd into the car and then threw a scratchy, heavy blanket on top of him. The driver pulled away rapidly, and Todd made a silent plea: *Let it be quick. And let me be brave.*

Relationship to Envy

Clarissa

September 19th

h ave you read any of this?" Standing at the threshold, Ruby waved her right hand, which gripped a stack of papers.

"Come in, Ruby. Hi, Angie."

"During the lulls, I've been online, googling Afghanistan, and the Taliban, and kidnapping."

Clarissa took the printouts without looking at them. "Google turns up a lot of stories that don't have anything to do with Todd. I'm trying to stay away from that."

"Well, maybe that explains some things."

"Ruby." Angie, chiding, pushed past Ruby and moved toward the kitchen. Clarissa, and finally Ruby, followed.

"Okay, I'm sorry," Ruby said. "I *am* sorry, Clarissa. But I'm also so frustrated. Read the top one. In eastern Afghanistan, where Dad is, the Taliban will pay $500,000 to get their hands on a Westerner. We can't match that, no way. Read the one under that. Two French hikers were kidnapped in what is supposed to be a safe area. Their bullet-riddled bodies were found a couple weeks later. No demands were ever made, no claim of responsibility. Who knows who had them? It's beyond chaos there. We can't sit here waiting. We're up against tough odds, and they've just gotten tougher."

"But we have Amin working on our behalf. And your father trusted—trusts—him." For slipping into past tense, Clarissa immediately hated herself.

"My God, Clarissa. Do we need the whole of the earth to be burning before we call in the fire department?"

"Ruby," Angie said again.

"Okay, okay." Ruby took a deep breath. "Look, we have to get on the same page somehow. Let's talk to Jack."

"I've never considered Jack to be my guide on how to proceed here."

"And I've never considered Bill mine."

Such thick lines were being drawn. "Let's check in with both of them, then," Clarissa said, "now that we have new developments on the ground. Jack first?"

"Great idea," Angie said quietly.

Ruby picked up the phone, put through the call, and put Jack on speaker. "I'm here with Clarissa, Jack. We both want to talk to you in light of this latest bunch of Afghan fatalities in the east, probably near where Dad is."

"Yes, I heard," came Jack's disembodied voice, "Actually, I was planning on calling you. We just got word that Todd is being moved."

"Moved? What does that mean?" Ruby asked.

"We don't know, exactly."

"Does this mean you know where they've been holding him?" Clarissa asked.

"Not precisely. No. But we've been following phone communications. That's why we know as much as we do."

"Moved? Oh, God." Ruby sucked in her breath. Her eyes began to tear.

"Look," Jack said, "this may be nothing. He's been moved several times already, don't forget. Don't draw any conclusions."

Clarissa sank into a chair as Ruby reached to the sink to get a glass of water. "You have no clues as to why?"

"None."

"Can our soldiers rescue him?" Ruby asked.

"First they have to find him, which is harder to do while his location is shifting. But say they can. Does this mean we have your okay to go ahead?"

"No."

Ruby spun toward Clarissa, her face a gathering of fury.

"Still no for now," Clarissa repeated, working to smooth her voice. "But we're calling Bill next. Then we'll get back to you. We'll be fast."

"Okay," Jack said. "I'll wait to hear from you."

Turning her back on the pressure of Ruby's stare, Clarissa called Bill's office. His secretary said he was out. "Can you have him call me? The minute he gets in?" Clarissa replaced the receiver, her hand shaking. The phone sat in the middle of the kitchen table, a betrayal of a space that should be for family and food and convivial conversation.

Ruby circled the kitchen, caged. "I don't want to wait."

"We're waiting," Angie said, her voice cool. "Sit down, Ruby."

Ruby stared fiercely at Angie for a moment, then obeyed. The three of them sat in silence. "I'll make tea," Clarissa said finally. She rose to fill the pot, set it to boil, and put fruit on the table, letting these sounds of feverish domesticity stand in for conversation.

Ruby's cell phone rang. She pulled it from her pocket, frowning. "I'm going to take this upstairs."

Clarissa was relieved to have her leave the room. She lifted her cup of tea and held the warm liquid against her lips, somehow not able to swallow, trying to imagine what it was like for Todd to be moved, how precisely they accomplished it, what he felt: fear, or desperation, or confidence.

"You okay?" Angie asked.

Clarissa had almost forgotten Angie. "Oh, God, I don't know," she said.

"I know. I'm sorry."

"So." Clarissa took a deep breath. "I hear you've had a . . . a sense of what should be done?"

Angie tipped her head. "I thought you didn't believe in that stuff."

Clarissa smiled slightly in acknowledgment. "But I suspect your insights are as valid as any Jack is offering."

"I get all kinds of feelings, actually, and I don't know how to interpret them. Last week I felt Ruby's dad was eating a bagel. An everything bagel, in fact. I didn't tell Ruby. I know that's impossible."

"Yes, I think you're right."

"So I'm not accurate here. But—" She hesitated. "I've had some bad dreams, to tell you the truth. And then, for the last day or two, I've felt better." She looked out Clarissa's kitchen window. "Maybe it's just wishful thinking."

An ambulance passed, its whine running between the brown-stones of Brooklyn, sending a chill down Clarissa's back that she tried to ignore. "There's a certain power in wishful thinking," she said. "I'll take it, in the absence of any real knowledge."

Angie reached out and touched Clarissa's hand. "Ruby is really a much more gentle person than she's been during this period."

"Hmm. I admire much about Ruby, but 'gentle' is not a word . . ."

"You know, she and her dad were together so long, just the two of them. When I moved in, at first Ruby was hard on me. I didn't know why, and then I realized she did not want to share her father with me. She was in charge. And she knew she was the center of her father's world."

"Then I came along."

"She wants to be the one who cares the most about her father."

Clarissa was moved by Angie's effort to navigate what little middle space remained between her and Ruby. "I get it, I do," she said. "I lost both my parents. It created a bond between my brother and me that—well, Mikey's still single. I waited a long time to marry. I think one of the reasons I could marry Todd was that he understood how that kind of sorrow rearranges your heart. It changes and complicates the way you love." She smoothed the wood of the kitchen table with her right hand. "I don't think Ruby has to be gentle. She has a certainty that, in honesty, I've never really had. But what I do believe is that we've made the right choices, until now. And by that, I mean the choices Todd would have asked of us."

"You may be right. Don't tell Ruby I said that, though."

"Gentle Ruby?"

Angie smiled. "You both have backbone," she said. "Someday—"

Before she could finish her sentence, the phone rang. Clarissa reached to grab it and heard Ruby moving quickly down the stairs toward the kitchen.

"Bill, hi. Thanks for calling back. We're afraid we have a problem. You heard about the American bomb that killed all those Afghans yesterday? Now Jack says they are moving Todd, and we—"

"Clarissa, Clarissa. Wait," Bill said.

"What?"

"I just got off the phone with Amin, Clarissa. I have news."

Admiral's Row

Danil

September 19th

he cradled in his hand the cell phone Joni had given him. He
tried to think of how he might begin the conversation. At
some point, the space of silence becomes its own country
with barrier fences, border patrols. He hadn't known it would be like
this. In the beginning, when he'd stopped contacting his mother, he'd
thought it would be for a week or two. By now it had turned into a
wide expanse that felt dangerous to cross.

On impulse, he dove his hand into the pile, pulling out a letter
from somewhere in the middle. He tore open the side of the envelope
and removed the page before he could think too much about it. He
read, skimming, letting his eyes leap over entire sections.

"Dear Dani, Last night for dinner I made . . . I saw Sasha last
week. She asked about you. . . . I love you, dear son. Piotr was a hero,
and I don't understand why you can't accept . . ."

He quickly refolded the letter and replaced it. He picked up the
most recent letter and held it in his hand for a moment, wavering.
On the street outside the abandoned building, a fire engine passed,
honking its horn. Somewhere beyond that, a dog barked in answer.

Danil felt safely contained within this crumbling room, protected from the world beyond.

He rearranged himself so that he was leaning against a solid part of the wall and opened the letter.

"Dear Dani, I wait for one of these letters to reach you. I will keep trying until I get through. I will keep repeating myself and hope one day you will get my letters, read them, and call.

"I wrote this before, but again I want to tell you that I'm thinking of selling the shop to a woman who owns a used bookstore fifty miles away. Her store is very different from mine, of course. She has what she called an 'online presence.' She says I could work for her half the year, so I could keep some income, but it would be a simpler, easier life. No more dashing after estate sales, stocking shelves, worrying about paying the store rent. Dani, I want to sell. Yvette is even starting to get used to it. But I won't sell until I hear from you; I don't want you to come looking and find me gone.

"I still don't understand the ways in which time alters our perception of life and events, how what seems so completely certain at one moment can become questionable and then false later on. It's as if we live under a constant delusion, and even what we discover to be truth is only another temporary delusion. Over and over again I get fooled; I believe in absolutes, I accept what I'm told. Perhaps this comes from a childhood in the Soviet Union. Perhaps it is simply my personal temperament.

"I know what I said was wrong, and I have something to confess: part of me knew from the start that you were right, but I couldn't acknowledge it, even to myself. Somehow I thought that accepting that Piotr had died in such a pointless way was like losing him all over again. But I know how hard that viewpoint must have been for you.

"Eventually, a drop hollows out a stone. You are that drop, Dani, even in your silence. Please call me. I will keep writing for as long as I can hold a pen, waiting for a response. Our Piotr has been dead long enough, and there's nothing I can do except make up wishes. You've been gone long enough, too, and I'm doing all I can to fix it."

Danil refolded the letter and replaced it in the envelope, waiting for a moment to make sure his voice wouldn't crack when he called. He was wrong to let it get so big. That, he decided, was the first thing he would tell her.

part four

For when they saw we were afraid,

how knowingly they played on every

fear—

so conned, we scarcely saw their

scorn,

hardly noticed as they took our

funds, our rights,

and tapped our phones, turned back

our clocks,

and then, to quell dissent, they

sent . . .

(but here the document is torn)

— ELEANOR WILNER

Seize in your being that which has

seized and broken you.

— ALAIN BADIOU

Najibullah

Letter to My Daughters IV

September 21st, 1996

m*y dear daughters, I'm sorry my conversation with each of you this afternoon had to be so painfully brief. But I was glad to find a way to call, to make sure your mother knows I am fine and strong and optimistic. I've listened as the Talibs took the south and the west, Kandahar and Herat. Rockets have cratered my garden. A window shattered in my hallway. A hole gapes in my ceiling. And now they have taken Surobi; they have the keys to Kabul. Yes, they sit thirty miles to the northeast, prowling at the outskirts of our city. In the distance, I hear the ring of rocket fire.*

Oh, Heelo, if I could have answered your question today with a long reply. "What does this mean for you?" you asked me, and I could only say, "I don't have much time on the phone; I need to talk to your sisters. Be strong and take care of your mother." Those words echo within me; I did not want those to be the last you heard from me today; you are the oldest, and you deserved a longer answer. If it had been possible, I would have told you: the moment is serious, but still I say, Heelo jan, soon the branches shall be filled with flowers, for I have noticed red buds on their tips.

It is not that I expect those who are sane to muster forces against those who are not at this eleventh hour. No, it is too late for that; my repeated appeals to international leaders have gone unheard, and now we will all pay the price, and they will one day say to you, "Your father was right."

But all is not lost. If it is Allah's will, I expect to rejoin you in less than a week. I've sent an urgent message to UN headquarters in New York. I told them: You promised me safe passage all those years ago. The promise was delayed, but it is time to keep it. I seek the immediate evacuation of myself; my younger brother, Shahpur Ahmadzai; and my bodyguard and my secretary, who have been with us for these long years. Thank you. I signed it: President Dr. Mohammed Najibullah Ahmadzai.

So far, no word.

But I wait, and I trust.

The boy Amin stays with me, though I've bade him go. "Back to your family," I told him. "You've done your job well. Now you do not want to be found with me."

"I will serve you chai until the UN comes to deliver you to the airport," he said, but by the way his eyes filled as he spoke, I knew he does not truly believe they will come for me.

I believe, though, my daughters. I believe.

On the strength of that belief, I twice refused Massoud's offers to spirit me away to the north of Afghanistan, to Panjshir. I do not trust him—in the end, he is an Islamist just like Rabbani. If the worst comes, these Taliban will capture me and then banish me from Afghanistan—I am of their blood, a fellow Pashtun, and they will do nothing worse than that. General Tokhi agrees with my assessment. My younger brother, your uncle, does not, I fear. Though he stays silent, when he looks at me, I see what is in his eyes. I do not allow such looks of fear in my own gaze now.

Paradise is a good place, my brother says, but the heart must be lacerated to get there. Those I have harmed, and this includes you by my absence, will never know how fiercely I wish I could stand before them—before you—and ask forgiveness. My daughters, I love you. I love your mother. I love my siblings, and send special greetings to my oldest sister, Saleha, my khoro, whom little Onie so resembles. I have missed you all almost to the limits of my endurance over these years. I am not afraid, and I will not say farewell. But just in case, I want you to know I am thankful for all I've had. Death on a full belly is better than a life of hunger.

I don't want—nor expect, if Allah wills—to depart this earth without being in your company again.

All my love, your

Najib

The Last Letters

Stela

September 24st

To: Mr. James Fairfield, Editor, Arts Beat

Dear Mr. Fairfield,

My name is Stela Sidorova, and I am writing to extend a personal invitation to you for an upcoming gallery opening and to give you a very good tip on a young artist whose work should be covered by the *New York Times* if you are to remain truly relevant in the art world today. His work is compassionate, textured, stimulating, and important. (Yes, I have looked at some of the descriptions you yourself have used in your columns.) It's street art making its way into galleries; it will be featured two weeks from now in the Rustlessend Gallery in the Chelsea area of Manhattan, and the artist himself will be there, actually painting on a gallery wall as if to simulate the work he does late at night outdoors. His work is a visually moving reminder to America of its place in the violent world that we inhabit and to which we contribute. He defies the law in creating it, but there is a reason for that. The work is dedicated to his brother, who was killed as a soldier in Afghanistan under murky circumstances that are still under investigation, or should be. (Information on this is difficult to obtain.) Therefore, he questions the legality of his own brother's death. He is articulate, and his story is compelling.

The artist's name is Danil Sidorov. I have held back that information until now because, yes, we are related. (He is my son, and it is my other son, Piotr, who died in Afghanistan.) But that is not the reason I am alerting you to this great opportunity. It is because too little of our art is this meaningful in so many contexts. Please send someone, a junior reporter if you must, or better, yourself. I will be there and will make sure Dani answers any questions you may have.

Thank you for your time, and sincerely,

Stela Sidorova

Dear Piotr, oh, dear Piotr,

I remember. I remember so much. I remember it all.

Those early years, the three of us a core of light that burned at the center of every day.

The Saturday morning that you and Dani went out after a rainstorm to play while I worked to clean the house and do the laundry. Then you appeared at the back door, both of you naked, covered with mud and laughing. For a second, I was angry, thinking of your dirty bodies tromping across my clean floor, but then I began to laugh, too. I lifted each of you in turn and carried you to the shower.

The day I took you boys to a neighboring farm to see the cows and goats, and one of the baby cows came up and tried to kiss you, grabbing gently onto your T-shirt. I was laughing, and you were, too, though you were also scared. I didn't notice that at first, but Dani did; he was the one who pulled you away.

The day you came home after that nasty little boy had bullied you. Your cheek was bruised. And you said when he hit you, you found you couldn't lift your arms to hit him back, that they froze in place, and you didn't know why. Finally, you were able to lift them, but only to shield yourself. And how angry Dani got on your behalf.

Remember how you called a hippopotamus a "cow-fish"? And how you used to believe if you waved your arms quickly enough, you could make a windstorm? And how you could burp on command? Remember the Easter of freak weather, when you and Dani hunted eggs in the snow? Remember when I got frightened because your voice sounded like you were sick, but it was because you'd inhaled the helium from a birthday-party balloon?

I want those moments back.

Of course I wouldn't be able to have them back even if you were still here now, a grown man, and of course I would still mourn their loss. But not with the bitterness I feel now.

I can't stand to have lost you.

Piotr, Dani is an artist now, and has his first gallery show in New York City in a few weeks. I wish so much that you could be there, but you will be there, because the work is dedicated to you. In fact, he signs each piece not with his own name but with "IMOP." It stands for "In Memory of Piotr." We had trouble after your death, Dani and I. I couldn't accept the truth. But Dani made me see it. He did it out of love for you, which I didn't understand at first, but you would have, I'm sure, even from the beginning.

There is nothing to match the way I love you and Dani. There is nothing to ease what I feel with you gone before me. I haven't been able to find a philosopher or poet whose words bring true comfort, though I keep opening the books, searching. I hope you can rest in peace, without any burden of pain, and that we can carry that pain for you. I want you to know, if there is any way for you to know, that you live on through Dani and me, and that you touched us deeply, and that we miss you beyond the power of words to say.

I love you, Piotr.

Mom

Going Home

Mandy

September 21st

mandy leaned over her suitcase, tucking in the few items she was bringing home as gifts. A Tajik hat for her brother. A scarf to give one sister, a small container of saffron for the other. For Jimmy, a string of lapis lazuli prayer beads and a note signed by six men he'd fought with who were still here; Hammon and Corporal Holder had helped her track them down. "It went so fast," she said.

"I'm just glad it went safely," Hammon answered. She hadn't seen him for three days, and no one had been able or willing to tell her when he would return, so she'd feared she'd have to depart without saying good-bye. He'd managed to show up half an hour before she had to head to the airport.

"You're going to be a little relieved to have me gone, I suspect. One less person to be responsible for."

"It's been no trouble at all."

"Now, that's not true." Mandy smiled. "How long do you think you'll stay here? Or is that classified?"

Hammon shrugged. "As long as there's work to do. Work that seems meaningful. So I think I'll be here when you come back."

Mandy started; she actually was thinking of returning, but she hadn't said that aloud yet. Was Hammon kidding, or had he somehow read her mind? She studied his face, which looked serious. "You really think Jimmy could come here and help you?"

"He'd be great here. He's talented with the computer stuff, and he understands the place, and he's got solid judgment about people."

Mandy considered Hammon's assessment. "I think that's true," she said. "But still . . . wouldn't he have to come face-to-face daily with the things he can't do anymore?"

"There are things all of us can't do. You'd never been here before, and you don't speak the language. Would you call your trip successful?"

Mandy sensed Hammon wasn't referring to the nurses' training or the supplies she had brought. He was asking something more elemental. In fact, at last, a process of forgiveness was starting to take hold in her: forgiveness for Jimmy, and for herself. But that was too personal and tentative to share. "I'm glad I got to see the first frame of what Jimmy saw," she said. "I made some connections that are important, at least to me. And I admit it's been good, in an odd way, to be in a place where tragedy isn't something to be denied. Nobody here is insisting I have a nice day."

The driver who would take her to the airport appeared at her door. Hammon held up a finger, signaling one more minute. "Ready?" Mandy zipped up the suitcase, and Hammon carried it out for her.

"What happened to Jimmy," Hammon said as they walked toward the car, "it could have happened to any of us."

"I know," Mandy said. "I'm sure you've had your close calls."

She stood on her toes to hug this friend of her son's, and then she leaned back to look him in the face. "One last question for now," she said. "Is Hammon your real name?"

He laughed. "Who wants to be google-able?"

"There's my answer."

"No, this is your answer: trust what you see, what you feel, and don't worry about insignificant details."

She smiled as she settled into the car.

"You give Jimmy my best when you talk to him," Hammon said through the open window. "In fact, every time you talk to him." Then he waved as she pulled away, heading to the airport and back home.

On the Way

Clarissa

September 22nd

C larissa leaned out toward the window, a blanket wrapped over her shoulders. She was on a military flight, surrounded by soldiers, still an hour and a half from Ramstein Air Base. A base she'd never heard of before yesterday but now would probably never forget. This was where she would be reunited with Todd. She believed he was there already; they'd been intentionally vague about that, but she imagined him showered, shaven, fed, and now sleeping. She herself couldn't sleep. Both she and Ruby had been able to speak to Todd, but briefly; he'd still been in Afghanistan then, in U.S. hands. That felt solid to her, but there'd been a tentative quality to the tone of the American official who had called her and then put Todd on the line for a few compressed minutes. She'd understood that he couldn't yet answer all the questions she had, and she couldn't yet share all the thoughts and emotions crowded inside her like unruly schoolchildren. It was as if nothing could truly be certain until he'd departed from Afghan soil.

The plan was for Todd to spend two days in Germany for debriefing and a physical checkup—there were injuries, she'd been told, but nothing too serious. And then they'd be flown home. She'd suggested to Ruby that they both go to Germany, but yesterday Ruby had called and said Clarissa should go alone; she would connect with her father later; it would only be a few more days anyway. It had been a generous gesture, one of reconciliation.

She'd been calm and strong all the way through this last part, except with Mikey an hour before she'd left to catch the flight.

"You did good, Clarissa."

She shook her head. "I'd let Todd lift the pain of those other losses, so when I thought I was going to have to go through it all again, I . . . you know."

"Grief is stubborn. It holds on a long time," Mikey said. "When you think it's over, something touches it off again. But you weren't like with Mom and Dad, Clari. If the worst had happened, you'd have found the resources."

She wasn't sure. She decided not to be too hard on herself now, though. Now was a time to feel gratitude—especially for Amin. He'd given her something she really, deep down, hadn't thought possible: a happy ending. Thinking about how close they'd come, she leaned against Mikey.

"I know," he murmured as he let her cry. "I know."

Arriving Home

Amin

September 22nd

he left directly before dawn and stopped only once, pulling the mat from the trunk to pray by the side of the road. He tried not to let his eagerness to get home make him rush through the praise of Allah, because it was surely Allah Himself who had cupped Amin in His hands this time and seen him through this venture. But except for the prayer, he sped as quickly as he could over the pockmarked roads that led from his uncle's home to his own. It was still early when he arrived. Though she'd been given no word as to when he might appear, his wife stood at the door as if she'd been expecting him, and he was not surprised to see her there. He lifted her palms to his face, smelling on her the scent of dawn, and of his home.

"And so, my wife of little faith," he said lightly.

"Congratulations, husband," she responded as she led him inside. "You have returned. You took a risk."

"Not such a risk."

She laughed. "Such confidence rides on your voice."

"I confess to a certain doubt at one point about whether Mr. Todd would agree to this compromise with his kidnappers," he said. "But I reminded myself that the past is not the present. Najib was asked to sneak from his own homeland. That's different."

"Except that a man's pride is as powerful as it is illogical," she said, pouring him a cup of *chai*. "It can lead him to embrace an unreasonable act or refuse a reasonable one."

"You speak not of me, of course, but of Najib and Mr. Todd," he said, allowing himself to smile.

She ran her fingers lightly along his arm. "And now, husband. Can we consider that whatever debt you thought you owed has been paid?"

"So you regard an infidel as adequate payment for an Afghan president?"

She shook her head. "To me, such calculations always seem to be the work of men, not women."

If he were a different sort of man, he thought, or if they were from a different country, he would laugh with a wide mouth and scoop his wife into his arms. She filled him with pride; she was strong and determined, and she would raise their children well in a place that tore its offspring from the ground by their roots and flung them into sharp-toothed canyons of fate. There were sorrows ahead, he was sure; there were always sorrows here. But with her, he could meet them. He drank deeply of the *chai*, controlling the leap of his heart within his chest.

She left him alone then, sensing in some way his need, and he sank onto a *toshak*. Mr. Todd—a thinner, weaker, limping Mr. Todd—had been both apologetic and grateful, and willing without question to do as Amin had promised the elders he would. He would leave immediately. He would never return. The elders could count this as a victory. There remained a much larger battle to be fought here, but someone else would fight it. Amin had been relieved.

"Crazy as it sounds," Mr. Todd had said, "I heard your voice sometimes. Telling me what to do."

Amin laughed. "And so you . . . ?"

"Did it." Mr. Todd smiled. "Mostly."

They'd shaken hands. Amin wondered if they would ever see one another again. Probably not—but neither would they forget.

One man is not the same as another. Success in one venture does not make up for horrible failure in another. And yet, in some way, this was a private commemoration. *Dear Najib*, Amin thought, *you were large and flawed and prophetic and bull-like. I admired you, and still I could not save you. I will never stop being sorry. But at least . . . at least there was this.*

conclusion

Cover him, cover him soon!

And with thick-set

Masses of memoried flowers—

Hide that red wet

Thing I must somehow forget.

— IVOR GURNEY

Najibullah

The Last Night

September 26th, 1996

*O*nly now has it fallen quiet, as if finally the day is finished, though in
fact it is almost midnight. Only now have the distant gunshots stilled,
the rockets stopped making exclamation points in the darkness. It is
not, however, a peaceful silence; this Amin feels deep within his body. It is the
hush of muscles tensed, breath contained, knees bent in readiness to pounce.

Both Najib and his brother are awake. They are in the room Najib uses
for welcoming visitors. Najib, standing, wears socks but no shoes and the
Afghan-style clothing he has favored here all along; his brother, who sits, is
dressed as if a Western man. Only one of the two bodyguards remains outside
the door. The other eloped into the warning night without explanation, and
no one has mentioned his disappearance. It is, at the moment, too small a detail to be of import.

Amin could go, too. His services are not required. Najib has barely eaten
for days; he won't want food now. And the brothers have chai enough to last
them until morning, if morning still comes. They do not need him. They are
as if in a bubble together, communicating with only a few words but with
enormous intimacy. They seem, in fact, to have forgotten his presence. But
Amin can't bring himself to depart.

"These men are illiterate," Shahpur says. "They are animals. They all believe their swords must be reddened."

"They are our Pashtun cousins," Najib insists.

"This is not a fairytale. These are Talibs. You are too smart to be fooled by them," Shahpur says. "You have cursed the mujahideen, but these fighters will make the mujahideen seem like princes."

"They have honor, I'm sure of it." Najib paces toward the window. "At least some. And besides, perhaps there is still time for . . ." His voice trails off, as if he himself can no longer believe his optimistic words. He drops into a chair, and his shoulders slump in a way Amin has not seen in all these years.

"Perhaps," Shahpur offers in a tone of appeasement, "they will put you on trial, hoping to legitimize their government in international eyes."

"You think they care about international eyes?" Then Najib straightens. "You remember when we organized the protest and threw eggs at Spiro Agnew? Perhaps they will throw eggs at me." He laughs, but it is not a Najib laugh. It is weaker.

"Those were more innocent times. We ourselves were more innocent."

"You want innocence?" Suddenly Najib grows animated. "Remember when we decorated the camels in Peshawar, you and I? Bells and ribbons! They made music when they walked, and Father said, 'There is no holiday. You have decorated them pointlessly.' But Mother said, 'A decorated camel is never pointless.'" Najib laughs, stronger this time. "Remember the game we used to play, trailing after Father as he wound through the old marketplace to visit his friend at the goldsmiths, or the man who sold spices? How we pretended to be invisible and convinced ourselves we were because he did such a good job of ignoring us? Finally he would turn and shoo us away, and we would giggle and run. We never tired of that game. Remember the light in the

Khyber Pass—oh, Shahpur—and the golden sand, and the way the dust would coat our skin? Magic. I used to hate to wash it off." He takes a deep breath, and his voice becomes quieter; Amin leans forward to hear. "Remember Mama's hands at the end, how they grew so soft and clumsy. But we held them, you and I, together that final night, Shahpur. Another ending, and we were together then as well."

"What's all this memory?" Shahpur asks, and he laughs, but his laughter sounds fearful.

"There are still things I can do; I can control my thoughts. I want to think of those times. You are given the task of helping me. Can you recite some lines of poetry Father taught us?"

"Now?" Shahpur spreads his hands helplessly. "I am honored to be your brother, but I have not your wit or willpower."

"All right, then, we'll make music. A thing they would forbid, those foolish boys. Join me, brother." Najib begins to play the arms of his chair as if they were drums, and he sings—at least it is intended as song, Amin knows, and meant to summon bravery. But it emerges as a wordless, wide-mouthed tune from deep in the belly, from a soul in sorrow. Shahpur drops his head into his hands, and Amin himself cannot bear it anymore.

He should have stepped forward then, out of the shadows. He should have offered an escape route again; the plan was no longer ready for immediate launching, but the two men might have followed him home and hidden there until something, something could have been done. He doesn't repeat his offer. The depth of his emotions, the complexity of the moment, and his undone plans defy him. This, then, is his failure. Unable to think or to see through the water of his eyes, he hurries into the night. He believes he has witnessed history enough.

Afterword

In the predawn hours of September 27th, 1996, Taliban rebels fought their way into Kabul and, while most Kabulis slept, overran the UN compound, pulling Dr. Mohammad Najibullah Ahmadzai and his brother outside. They castrated and tortured Najibullah, dragging him behind a car through Kabul streets before hanging him from a concrete post in Aryana Square, in front of the city's most luxurious hotel. Residents found his mutilated, bloated, and blood-soaked body the next morning, with rolled-up Afghani bills stuck in his nose and mouth and between his fingers, his brother hanging beside him. Their bodies remained on display for two days.

Najibullah spent ten years, from 1965 to 1975, getting his medical degree from Kabul University. During that time, he was jailed twice for political activities. In 1980, he was appointed head of KHAD, the secret police. Under his leadership, thousands of Afghans were arrested, tortured, and executed. Appointed President of Afghanistan in 1985, he oversaw the withdrawal of Soviet soldiers in 1989. He continued to rule Afghanistan until April 1992, when he agreed to step down as part of a UN-brokered agreement that involved him handing over power to an interim government and leaving the country. But before he could depart, Uzbek warlord Abdul Rashid Dostum, his former ally, blocked his safe passage.

Burhanuddin Rabbani became president, with Ahmed Shah Massoud as military chief. For the four years and five months before the Taliban takeover, the United Nations gave Najibullah refuge in Kabul while Afghans turned their weapons on each other, destroying large sections of the capital city and killing some fifty thousand people.

Massoud was murdered in September 2001, days before the events of 9/11, by two men posing as journalists who had hidden explosives in a camera and a battery-pack belt.

Rabbani died ten years later, in September 2011 in another suicide-bomb attack. This one involved two men claiming to be Taliban representatives, one of whom had explosives hidden in his turban.

Dostum has managed to revise or reverse his political views in keeping with the time, at one point serving under President Karzai as a deputy defense minister.

After Najibullah's death, his wife and daughters continued to live quietly in exile in Delhi. In November 1998, his brother-in-law Mohammed Hashim Bakhtiari, who had condemned the Taliban for killing the former president, was gunned down outside his home in a suburb of Peshawar, northwest Pakistan. No one was ever charged with the murder.

"Destiny is a saddled ass; he goes where you lead him."

Acknowledgments

Deepest thanks to:

Marly Rusoff, Michael Radulescu and
   the Marly Rusoff Literary Agency

Fred Ramey, Greg Michalson,
   Caitlin Hamilton Summie and
   the unparalleled Unbridled team

Blue Mountain Center

Turkey Mountain Cove retreat

Readers Susan Ito and Barbara Fischkin

First reader Cheney Orr, as well as Daylon,
   Briana and David Orr,
   my constant inspiration.

Rupert and Arra Hamilton

Matthew Hamilton

For expressing gratitude, words seem frail.